THE UNEXPECTED *Gift*

Can an unexpected gift change your life?

The Unexpected Gift
Book 1 in the Unexpected series

COPYRIGHT

Published by DL Gallie Author

First published 30th March 2019 in the Calendar Men series as 'December'

Second Edition, 3rd November 2019

Edited by Karen Hrdlicka, Barren Acres Editing

Cover Design by Dana Leah of Designs by Dana

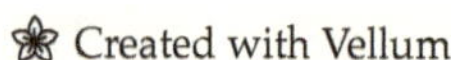 Created with Vellum

Could an unexpected gift change your life?

I hate Christmas.
I'm known as the Grinch amongst my friends and co-workers, but most don't know why. Christmas ruins lives or at least mine.

When the annual Christmas toy drive brings in a new member, something, well someone, crashes into me and I offer to help in a more hands-on way. Shocking everyone.

Why?
Marlee Adams.

There's something about her. She defrosts my frozen heart and life and Christmas become less bleak. It might be her never-ending legs and what they lead to, or it could her generous heart and infectious smile.

Marlee is my unexpected gift and exactly what I need to remember all the things good about this holiday...I just didn't know it yet.

THE UNEXPECTED SERIES

The Unexpected Gift

The Unexpected Letter

The Unexpected Package

The Unexpected Connection

ALSO BY DL GALLIE

THE CASTAWAY GROVE COLLECTION

Love has arrived in the Grove

Oasis

Unequivocal Love

Five Words

Broken Rules - coming mid / late 2020

…and a few more as well.

THE LIQUOR CABINET SERIES

Liquor has never been so disturbingly saucy

Malt Me (Book 1)

Tequila Healing (Book 2)

Wine Not (Book 3)

The Final Shot (Book 4)

The Liquor Cabinet: Series boxset

STAND ALONES

Out of Nowhere

Antecedent

Seven Nights

Falling for Dr. Kelly, a Falling novel

Falling for Dr. Knight, a Falling novel - coming May 2020

Doc Steel - coming June 2020

The Dirty Dozen: Alpha edition

The Rule Breaker Anthology - coming soon

In the Dark of Night anthology (only available in paperback directly from me)

Titanic Tales, a charity anthology (no longer available)

Gone Coastal, a sizzling summer beach anthology (no longer available)

Leave Me Breathless: The Lilac Collection (no longer available)

A NOTE FROM THE AUTHOR

This book was originally published n March 2019 as December, book 12 in the Calendar Men series.

It is the same story but this version has a new title and an extended epilogue giving you a peek into Gage and Marlee's life after the original epilogue.

To **Chloe**, *thank you for everything*

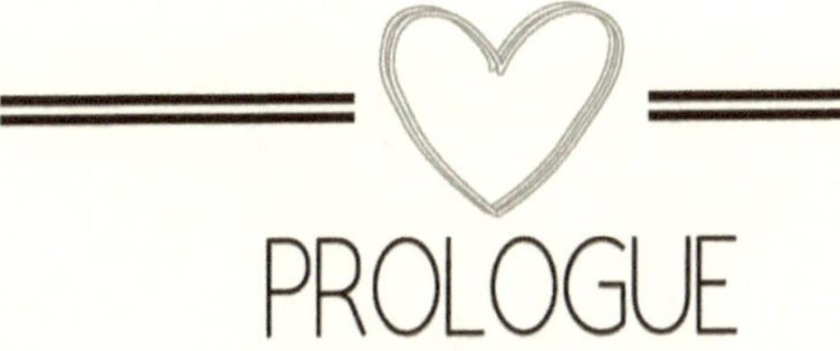

PROLOGUE

There was a point in time when I loved Christmas. The snow, the cookies, the songs, the tree; I loved it all. Then one year, my world shattered and I hated everything about it.

One Christmas I met someone and everything shifted. December and Christmas became the most magical time of year again for me. Who knew the gift of love had the power to change the course of my life?

This is the story of my unexpected gift.

CHAPTER 1

...December 20th, 1998
...twenty years ago

THE SNOW WAS LATE ARRIVING THIS YEAR; MA WAS WORRIED that there would be none for Christmas. It was already December and only a few flakes had fallen, which was highly unusual for Chicago. The air outside was chilly; the sky was gray, indicating that snow wouldn't be too far away, so I started to get excited for the impending snow-fall. I'd never had a Christmas with no snow; that would be weird, but also awesome at the same time. I don't know how those in Australia do it. We'd just learned about Australia in geography class; when I'm big, I want to go there and ride a kangaroo.

I'm on the floor in the living room, sitting by the fire playing with my trucks, when Dad comes stumbling in, he's drunk…this has been happening more often lately. Even though I'm only ten, I can't remember the last time he came home sober. It all started going downhill rapidly when he lost his job at the factory three months ago. I don't know how Ma puts up with him, but she loves him unconditionally. The wind outside is howling and the air blowing in the open door is freezing. "Ma, I think it's gonna snow," I excitedly say, jumping up to look out the door that Dad has left open.

Before I make it outside, Dad reaches out and grabs me by the scruff of the neck. "Where you going, Son?" he slurs.

"Outside to see the snow fall."

"Don't be such a pussy. It ain't gonna snow 'til later, didn't your Ma teach you nothin?" He shoves me to the side and walks into the kitchen. He swings open the fridge door and growls, "Where's my beer, woman?"

"At the store, dear," Ma replies. "Gage and I are going to run out just as soon as the cookies for the church bake sale are done."

"What the hell did you do all day? I want a beer now."

"You'll just have to wait. The world doesn't revolve around you, dear husband," Ma says in reply, placing a gentle kiss on his cheek.

Dad grins at Ma and it's nice to see his features soften and his eyes reflect love toward her; that is until he opens his mouth again. "I remember a time when this house was spotless. There was always beer in the fridge. Dinner would be in the oven waiting for me when I got home."

"Times change, dear." The oven timer dings. "Look at that, I can head to the store in a few moments and get you your precious beer." She looks over to me. "Gage, go and put your shoes on and grab our coats, please. As soon as I have placed these on the cooling rack we can go."

"Yes, Ma," I say, beginning to pack up my toys.

"Ma, you can drop me at The Grand and pick me up when you're done," Dad interjects, completely ignoring me. The Grand is the local pub closest to where we live, it's Dad's second home. Which is what I prefer, if he's not ignoring me, he's picking on me—"You're too small, Son. You're too tall, boy. You're such a pussy. You're a disgrace," that's my favorite one. There's no pleasing him.

"Yes, dear," Ma agrees, as she begins to place the cookies on the cooling rack. Ma placates him all the time. I may only be ten, but I know he treats her like shit. If I ever get a wife, I'll never treat her like he treats Ma. Sometimes I wish he was dead, but I know that would crush Ma, she loves him unconditionally; assholeness and all.

Ten minutes later, we head out and walk to the car. It's freezing. I look to the sky and see it's grayer than before and gloomy, there's definitely snow coming tonight. I can feel it in my bones. With a pep in my step at the impending snow, I climb into the back seat of Ma's Volvo and put my seat belt on.

Ma has just put her belt on when Dad bellows, "Put the heater on, woman!"

"It is, dear," she pats him on the thigh and they lovingly smile at one another, "it just takes a while to warm up."

Dad growls and mumbles to himself. The car is silent on the five-minute trip to The Grand. Dad is opening the door to jump out before Ma has even stopped. "I'll make my own way home," he says to Ma, as he climbs out. He slams the door shut and waddles his fat ass into the pub.

"Have a good time, dear," Ma cheerfully says, even though Dad doesn't hear because he's long gone.

Ma waits until Dad is inside and then pulls away from the curb. We drive up to a red light and she turns the radio on. A Christmas song is playing. Ma and I sing along with it. When the song finishes, I ask, "Ma, who sang that? It's my favorite Christmas song."

"It's called 'Winter Wonderland' and it's sung by Dean Martin. And guess what, buddy?"

"What?" I eagerly reply.

"It's my favorite too."

With a smile on my face, I sit back in my seat and stare out the window, when all of a sudden it starts to snow. "Look, Ma, it's snowing."

"Well, look at that, it is too. It's a Christmas miracle."

We pull up at the mall and climb out. Looking up to the sky, I let the snowflakes fall on my face. "Quick, let's get this done and we can get home and watch the snow fall."

"There's no rush," she says, grabbing my hand and squeezing it like she always does. Lifting my head, I look up at Ma. She is beautiful. Curly golden blonde hair that goes to her shoulders. Vivid blue eyes, just like mine, and a smile that lights up her face.

"Yes, there is, because tonight's the night," I excitedly say, "the snow is here."

Tugging on Ma's hand, I pull us toward the stores. As we enter the mall, she looks down at me and gives me a smile; it's a smile I will always remember. I grin back up at her and link my fingers with hers. *I love my Ma so much.*

As soon as we are inside, I hear Christmas music. I can smell roasted chestnuts. People are chattering. Santa is yelling, "HO! HO! HO!" There's a huge tree and everything is adorned in either tinsel or Christmas lights. It's magical. It's wonderful. It's Christmassy.

We quickly get what we need, Pa's beer included, and then we make our way back to the car. We load the shopping into the trunk and climb in. Ma lets me sit in the front this time, I like sitting up front, you can see so much more from here.

We pull out onto the main road and head toward home. We turn the radio back on and catch the tail end of a song. I'm eagerly awaiting the next song when disaster strikes. We are around the corner from home when Ma hits a patch of black ice and she loses control. The car spins and spins, there's no stopping it; we are out of control. The car crosses the centerline and we veer into oncoming traffic, there's a truck coming straight at us. There's nothing we can do.

The sound of the two vehicles colliding is deafening. Metal crunching. Glass shattering. Screaming from both Ma and me. Ma screams in a way I will never forget. Up until this moment, I had never heard anything like it before. When the car finally stops moving, my eyes open, I hadn't realized I had closed them. Blinking a few times, my vision comes back. Looking over my body, I sigh when

I realize I'm unhurt, even though my head is bleeding furiously. Glancing over to Ma, my eyes immediately fill with tears and my heart shatters into a million tiny fragments, just like the windshield. Her hair is no longer golden and beautiful, it's matted and stained dark red. Her face is covered in blood. Her arm is bent the wrong way and her eyes…her eyes are wide open and vacant. It looks like she's staring at me but she's not seeing me; she doesn't seeing anything anymore. Her eyes are no longer vivid blue but a dull gray. Until the day I die, I will never forget that vacant, blank look staring back at me, that image will forever be etched in my mind.

A scream erupts from me when I realize that Ma is dead, and I'll be left alone…with him. I try and move but my seat belt is cutting into me and I'm trapped. Panic begins to set in and I start screaming and shouting. The fear coasting through me causes my vision to blur. The last thing I remember before I pass out is Ma and her vacant gaze staring back at me.

The next time I wake up, the sun is rising and I'm in a hospital bed. Pa is sitting in the chair next to me, he reeks of beer and cigarette smoke. His eyes are red-rimmed, I don't know of it's from the booze or over Ma. When he notices I'm awake, he sadly smiles at me. "You're awake. Let's go."

He doesn't ask how I am.

He doesn't offer me any sympathy at all.

He's indifferent…he's Dad.

He signs my discharge papers and we make our way home…silently…just the two of us.

When we arrive home, I look to the counter and see the

remnants of Ma's baking from yesterday, and it's in that moment, it all comes crashing back into me.

I'm all alone now.

The one person in this world who cared for me and love me unconditionally is gone...this Christmas will forever be known as the one that ruined my life.

CHAPTER 2

…December 3rd, 2018
…current day

THE SOUND OF CHRISTMAS MUSIC RINGS THROUGH MY EARS AS I quicken my pace through the food court and back to the office. "I fucking hate Christmas," I mumble to myself as I round the Christmas tree in the foyer. Thankfully the elevator is there and I climb into the waiting car. The doors close and I smile as the Christmas music fades, and I'm now listening to the drab elevator music as I ride up to WFOX-FM. I'm the marketing director and have been here for coming on fours years now. Seriously, I will take drab elevator music over Christmas tunes any day. Hell, I'd even take silence over Christmas tunes, anything to do with Christmas sucks ass.

Thank God Christmas only comes around once a year, but must all the major retailers start with that shit right after Halloween? It's like they are trying to punish me. Trying to make me remember that fateful day earlier and earlier each year.

The elevator doors open and I step out into the foyer of WFOX-FM and I crash—literally—into a warm svelte body. Glancing over, I see an angel before me. Her eyes are hypnotizing, her legs go on and on, and her ass, which my hand is currently resting on, is phenomenal. "Shit, I'm so sorry. Are you okay?"

"Umm, yeah, I'm fine, but if you could kindly remove your hand from my ass that would be great," she huskily says, her eyes fused to mine. She swallows deeply as her eyes roam over my face.

"Shit, sorry," I say, *No, I'm not*, as I remove my hand from her perfect ass. Pulling her up into a standing position. My eyes subtly rake over her body. Her oh-so-fucking-fine body. My eyes eventually land on her face and I notice her cheeks are pink—pink with desire. When she realizes that I caught her checking me out, her cheeks darken further, and I can't help but smirk.

"I'm so sorry about that..." I pause, willing with my eyes, hoping she will offer me her name.

"Marlee Adams," she says with a smile that lights up her face, reminding me of Ma, when she'd smile at me.

"Pleasure to crash into you, Marlee, I'm Gage

Grainger." I stretch out my hand for her to take, and as soon as her soft delicate palm touches mine, I'm a goner.

"Nice to meet you, Gage." My eyes rake over her body once again, and I decide I need to have this woman writhing in pleasure beneath me. I raise my eyebrows suggestively and notice her swallow deeply. With a smirk, I ask, "Can I help you at all?"

"I'm here about the WFOX-FM charity toy drive," she cheerfully says.

Fucking Christmas, I think to myself as I plaster on a fake smile, the desire of wanting to be with her dwindling at the mention of Christmas, toys, cheer, and all that Christmassy bullshit. "You'd be after Kasey and Chelle, let me escort you to them."

"Thank you. I've been thrown into this at the last minute. Hence why I'm in a fluster right now."

"Here I was thinking you were in a fluster due to me," I playfully reply.

She looks up to me and once again, her cheeks darken and she swallows deeply.

"I...umm, ahh..."

"I'm joking, Marlee." She visibly relaxes at my reply. "Sort of," I quickly add.

"And will you be assisting us with this year's drive?"

Before my brain registers what I'm saying, I blurt out, "Of course, I am." *What the fuck, Grainger?* I internally scold myself, but when I see the smile light up Marlee's face, I think maybe it might work in my favor. Work closely with her. Wine her. Dine her. Unwrap her, then fuck her. I'm currently thinking about her legs wrapped around my head while I feast on her pussy; my cock likes these thoughts as it twitches in my pants.

Working with this sexy little minx might be just what I need to keep me occupied this Christmas. Maybe, this won't be so bad after all. If only I knew how fucked—and not in the good, naked, sweating, moaning way—I was about to become.

CHAPTER 3

"Knock, knock," I announce, as I walk into Kasey and Chelle's office. Chelle turns around and my eyes drop to her big pregnant belly. "WOW, look how big you are now!" I say.

"Just what every pregnant lady wants to hear," she snorts, dropping down into her seat and grabbing a piece of licorice from the huge container on her desk. "What can I do for you, Grainger?"

"This," I point to Marlee behind me, "is Marlee Adams, here about the charity toy drive."

"Shit," Kasey says, sitting up suddenly, while Chelle leans back and rests her hand on her belly. With a smile

Kasey apologizes, "I totally forgot that was today. My brain is all over the place." Chelle looks to Kasey, and smart-assly asks. "What's your excuse for forgetting, Kase?"

Kasey sticks out her tongue at Chelle. Marlee giggles, she has a gorgeous laugh that lights up her face.

"You're allowed. You are growing a tiny little person inside of you," Marlee says. "Gage here has offered to help, I can coordinate with him, if that's easier?"

Both Kasey and Chelle's heads snap toward me before Kasey says, "You did what, Mr. 'I hate Christmas and everything that goes with it' Grainger? Did you hit your head? Or has your body being taken over by aliens?"

"Very not funny. Just because I'm not a fan of Christmas, doesn't mean I can't help out and do something for charity."

Chelle looks at me suspiciously. "Gage, I've run this drive for the past four years. Not once have you offered to physically help. Not once. Sure, you chuck a ton of cash into the gift kitty, but actually offering of help? Nope. Something's..." She drifts off when her eyes land on Marlee and then she points her licorice stick at me. "I'm onto you, Grainger." She turns to Marlee. "Sorry about that...and him. I'm Chelle and I'll be the liaison with this. I have worked on this since I started here at WFOX-FM and just because I look like this," she flicks her hands up and around her belly, "doesn't mean I can't do it. Thankfully this year, I have Kasey and you assisting me...and by the looks of things, now Gage too."

"I'm sorry if I offended you," Marlee says. "I just thought...you know what, never mind. Let's start again."

She steps around me and in front of Chelle's desk. "Kasey. Chelle, I'm Marlee Adams, here to assist you with the charity toy drive. I'm excited to work with you both." She looks over her shoulder at me. "And you too Gage." The way she looks at me stirs something within me.

"Nice to meet you, Marlee. We are excited to work with you too. I've got some great ideas for this year's drive and I cannot wait to get started." Chelle looks to me. "Grainger, get out of my office. I'll summon you if and when I need your grinchy assistance."

"There's the snarky baby mama we all know and love." She flips me the bird and I laugh as I walk out of her office. I duck my head back in. "Nice to meet you, Marlee." I wink at her. "Later, Kase…Chelle." I quickly leave before anyone has a chance to reply.

With a grin on my face and a pep in my step, I walk back to my office and can't decide if I'll fuck Marlee before, during, or after the drive. All three would be great, but if I fuck this drive up, Kasey and Chelle will have my balls on a silver platter. Kasey I can handle, but Chelle, she's scary at the best of times, but when she's pregnant, she makes Bigfoot look like a fucking teddy bear.

Stopping in the breakroom, I make myself a double espresso and head back to my office. I've just sat down at my desk when the phone rings. Picking it up, I answer with the company greeting, "WFOX-FM this is Gage."

"Gage, Son, it's Dad." Comes across the line.

I freeze *Fuck, what does he want?* "Dad." That's all I offer, this man doesn't deserve anything from me. Not after the way he treated me after Ma died.

"Gage, I'm sick. I have liver cancer."

"So, the beers finally caught up with you," I sarcastically reply. Rubbing my temples and closing my eyes in frustration.

"Please, Son, I'm try…"

"No, Dad, you don't get to make amends on your deathbed. You've had years to make up for my shitty childhood. Years." I pause and take a deep breath. "You weren't the only one who lost Ma that day, I did too. I lost the one person who loved me unconditionally. Sooo many times, I wished it was you who had died and that I still had her with me. Well, I guess I'll finally get my wish that you were dead, but it won't bring her back. I'll never get her back. Look, I'm sorry you're sick, but it's too little to late. I have to get back to work." Without letting him reply, I slam the phone down. Thankful that he called the office line and I could slam the phone down, hitting a button on a screen just isn't as satisfying. There's nothing better than slamming the phone down in frustration. Yes, there is, fucking in frustration. My mind drifts to Marlee…I'm fucking her from behind, her body pressed to my desk, her ass in the air. "Fuck." I mumble to myself as my cock thickens within my pants at my vivid thoughts.

Leaning back in my chair, I adjust my cock and spin around to gaze out the window. The sky is gray and dreary, it's going to snow today. Sadly, I smile, wishing Ma was here. I sit and stare at my reflection in the window and think of Ma. As if on cue, it begins to snow.

From behind me I hear an angelic voice say, "I knew it was going to snow today. The sky was the right shade of gray."

Spinning my chair around, I find Marlee standing in

my office doorway. Once again, my eyes devour her body, and my cock twitches within my pants. I'm ever so thankful to have a desk in front of me right now. *Down boy,* I subconsciously say. "I was just thinking the same thing, and then BAM, the snow began to fall."

She walks into my office and takes a seat in the chair across from me. "My grandpa taught me to predict the snow."

"My Ma taught me," I offer.

We silently stare at one another over my desk. Our eyes boring into each other. Marlee smiles and it lights up her face, and surprisingly, it warms my heart AND I find myself returning her smile.

"Gage." "Marlee." We both say at the same time before we both laugh.

"You go first," she says before I get a chance to.

"I was wondering if you'd..." Suddenly, I'm nervous, this doesn't happen to me around women. I'm usually slick and have them eating out of my hand, but the woman sitting across from me unnerves me like no one ever before. "Would you like to grab a drink with me?"

"Ohh, ummm..."

"It's fine if you don't, I just thought...no never mind."

"You thought what?" she asks.

"It's all good, don't worry about it. What did you want to ask me?"

She shakes her head and begins to stand up. "It's fine. I'll speak to you soon."

Before I have a chance to reply, she walks out of my office.

Pushing back my chair, I let out a frustrated sigh. Lifting my hands, I rub my temples and close my eyes. A

vision of Marlee appears before me and I find myself grinning goofily.

Did I sense a hint of sadness when I didn't ask her out?

Or is it just my dick wishing so?

What is this woman doing to me?

CHAPTER 4

For the rest of the afternoon, my mind is a jumbled mess. Ma. Dad. Marlee. My mind flits between the three of them, but mostly my mind wanders to Marlee 'Oh so sexy' Adams and the wickedly sexy things I want to do to her body.

I'm staring out the window at the snow falling, when there's a knock at my door. Spinning around, I see Kasey. "What up, Buttercup?" I say with a smirk because I know she hates it when I call her Buttercup.

"I'm going to ignore that greeting and get straight to it. DO NOT FUCK AND CHUCK MARLEE ADAMS. Got it?"

"What says I want to?" I snap in reply, and wonder how the hell Kasey knows that I really, really want to.

"Don't play dumb, Grainger. One, you hate Christmas and now you're willingly offering to help with this toy drive. Two, I saw you eye-fucking her when we were in Chelle's office just now. And C, I know you Gage Grainger."

"You do not know me." She pops her hand on her hip and eyeballs me. "Okay, maybe you do know me, but—"

"I wasn't finished. Four," she raises her fingers indicating the number, "she is totally your type. And lastly, she's sexy as sin and you'd look cute together. **IF** you decide to go after her, don't do it in your usual wham-bam-thank-you-ma'am way. Woo her. Fall for her. Have a relationship with her, as your friend, I want you to be happy and have a love like Kody and I."

My eyes snap up to hers. "Love doesn't exist." I lick my lip and shake my head. "Not in my life anyway."

"Gage, not all relationships are like your parents'."

"No, don't bring my parents into this. Besides, this has nothing to do with them. I'm just not wired to fall in love."

She ignores me and continues, "When you find 'the one,' it's perfect in every imaginable way. They are the first thing you think of in the morning, and they are your last thought before you drift off to sleep. They do little things that mean nothing to an outsider, but everything to you. Their smile penetrates deep into your soul. Their presence is felt before you see them. Sure, they'll piss you off and you'll want to smother them with a pillow while they are sleeping, but at the end of the day, they are your other half. You feel lost when they are away from you. It's like you cannot exist without them. Without them, you are empty. You are miserable. And Gage, you are empty, miserable, and lost." She pauses and then adds, "And a fucking Grinch."

"Am not. I'm just…" I scoff in reply, but Kasey has hit the nail on the head, I am miserable. I'm lonely. I'm a grump, no, I'm a downright asshole. "I'm scared," I mumble.

"Scared of what?" Kasey asks, as she comes around my desk and leans against the wood.

"What if I'm like him?"

"Gage." She reaches over and squeezes my arm. "I'm sure you are nothing like him. You are kind. Sure, you're an asshole at times, but underneath it all, you are pretty great. I guarantee there is someone out there waiting for you to swoop in and woo them."

"Yeah. Nah. Maybe. Who knows? Maybe I'm destined to be alone and cranky for something that I did in a past life."

"I call bullshit on that, Grainger." She stands up and walks out of my office. She reaches the door and looks back at me. "She asked about you."

"Who did?"

"You know who I'm talking about." And with that, she leaves. Leaving me to ponder what Marlee asked them in regard to me, and more importantly, what Kasey and Chelle told her about me…not that I care.

"Bye, Buttercup!" I shout, and I faintly hear her say, "Asshole."

Leaning back in my chair, I stare out the window again and wonder if maybe she's right, maybe I do deserve to be happy and all that shit. As I sit and watch the snow falling, my mind drifts back to a happy memory from my child-hood, the last Christmas that Ma was alive…

…December 1st, 1998

Ma and I had just finished decorating the tree. All there was left was to place the angel on the top. I was getting too big for Ma to lift me up anymore, so she dragged over a chair from the dining room table. "Up you go, Gage," she said, her eyes bright and loving. She handed me the angel and I held it carefully in my hands. The angel's material was so soft and delicate. I was scared I was going to drop her. I had never held her by myself before; I'd always had Ma helping me. I was so nervous, I didn't want to break her. Closing my eyes, I took a deep breath and climbed up onto the chair. The tree before me felt huge, I was so little in comparison. I lifted my arms but I couldn't quite reach. I lifted onto my tippy-toes but I was still too short. All of the sudden, there was a hand on my shoulder and I heard Dad's voice from behind me, "Let me help, Son."

I gasped in utter shock; Dad was nice to me. Dad was sober. Moments like this didn't happen often lately. I looked over to Mu and she shrugged her shoulders at me and smiled. This smile lit her eyes up. It was moments like this that Ma loved. "Thanks," I said, offering the angel to Dad so he could place it on top, but he didn't take it. He wrapped his arms around my legs and lifted me up so I could put the angle on top of the tree.

After that, the three of us sat around the fire laughing and being a family; a happy family. We ate Christmas cookies. Ma made hot chocolate with marshmallows, it was the perfect Christmas moment in my ten-year-old mind.

• • •

As the memory fades, I stand up and walk over to my office window. Resting my forehead on the cool glass, I look out at the decorated tree below in the atrium of the building and smile. Christmas wasn't always bad. Turning around and leaning against the glass, I think to myself, *Maybe it's time to make some new Christmas memories...happy Christmas memories.*

After leaving the office, I stop in at the local Jewel-Osco to grab a few things for dinner. I'm in the meat section, trying to decide between steak and pork chops when the hairs on the back of my neck stand on end, and it's not from the cold of the meat case but because someone is approaching. Looking up, I see Marlee pushing her cart and walking toward me *This must be that sixth sense feeling that Kasey mentioned earlier*, I think as I watch her. She hasn't seen me yet, but I take the time to look at her. She's about my height, sexy as sin legs—that, once again, I'm currently imagining wrapped around my head—gorgeous tits, and an angelic face. She looks up and when our eyes connect, she smiles. This smile shoots straight to my heart, instantly kick-starting it.

"Hey there," she casually says.

"Hey," I reply.

We both fall silent, it's kind of awkward but at the same time not.

We are staring intently at one another, the air around us prickling. "Marlee, would you like to have a drink with me?"

She licks her bottom lip before chewing on it, thinking over my question. "I think I'd like that. When?"

"Now?"

CHAPTER 5

Now, what the hell, Grainger? This woman causes me to speak before I think. Next thing I know, I'll be asking her to carry my babies.

"Sure, why not?" she happily says, and her reply swells my heart. *Man, I sound like a lovesick fool.*

We both abandon our carts and head outside. "Where should we go?" I ask her.

"There's a new wine bar that recently opened nearby, I've been wanting to try it out."

"Wine isn't normally my thing, but sure, wine not." She laughs at my corny joke and her laugh is divine. "Would you like a lift?"

"That'd be great since I walked here."

Offering her my elbow, she links her arm though and we walk in silence to my car. Both of us not so subtly checking the other out. Pressing the key fob in my pocket, my car unlocks.

"Holy shit, this is your car?" she asks, her eyes bulging open at my car. I nod my head, but before I can say anything she says, "Is this the Audi A5 coupe?"

Shaking my head, I correct, "No, it's an R8." It's a total turn-on that she knows about cars.

She squeals with delight as she rounds the passenger side and climbs in. When I open my door, I swear I hear her moaning, and my mind flits to her riding me. Her head thrown back in ecstasy, she moans and writhes in pleasure, as we make sweet, sweet love. Rearranging my junk, I climb into the driver's seat. She looks over at me and smiles. "I've always wanted an R8 Spyder, but that's a pipe dream for me."

"Never say never," I offer in reply, as I start the ignition and drive toward the wine bar.

Ten minutes later, I pull into the parking lot behind the wine bar. On the drive over, I find out that Marlee has worked for *Chicago Hopes of Kids* for the last four months, prior to that she attended University of Illinois at Urbana-Champaign to complete her Master of Social Work, Leadership & Social Change Concentration degree. Listening to her talk about her work is mesmerizing. She loves what she does, and I can tell she really cares about the kids and their future.

As we walk into the bar and approach the hostess stand, she asks, "And what about you, Gage? Tell me about you?"

Thankfully I'm given a reprieve when the hostess

appears out of nowhere. "Welcome to Bin 501, table for two?"

"Yes, please," we both say at once. Glancing at each other, we both laugh.

"Follow me," the hostess replies, stepping to the side, I allow Marlee to go first. It is the gentlemanly thing to do after all, but more importantly, I can check out her ass. She's currently wearing jeans that accentuate her curves and a charcoal, off the shoulder sweater that makes her blue eyes pop.

We are seated toward the back of the bar, in a quiet area. Taking a seat across from Marlee, she grabs the menu and looks over it while I continue to check her out. As I do so, Kasey's words from earlier play in my mind about Marlee asking about me.

I'm snapped back to reality when another waitress appears. "Welcome to Bin 501, my name is Amy, and I'll be your server this evening. Can I start you with some drinks?"

Before I have a chance to reply, Marlee answers, "Can I grab a glass of Verdelho, please?"

"Ver-whato?" I ask.

Marlee smiles and lets out a throaty, heartfelt laugh, and I find myself grinning back at her. "Verdelho. It's white wine with floral notes and a fruity aroma."

"You lost me at white," I playfully reply. Turning to the waitress I add, "Make it a bottle."

Marlee smiles at me, her smile punches me right in the chest. I haven't ever had a reaction like this to a woman before, and again Kasey's conversation from earlier pops into my head. *Their smile penetrates deep into your soul.*

"Gage?" Hearing her snaps me back to the present.

"Sorry, what was that?"

"I asked about you. I've told you a lot about me, it's your turn now."

This is where I clam up and become uncomfortable. I'm not a fan of talking about my childhood—my shitty, sad childhood—so I answer how I always do. "There's not much to tell, really. I also attended U. Of I. where I completed my Master of Science in Strategic Brand Communication degree and soon after graduation, landed my marketing job at WFOX-FM. I stepped into the director's role eighteen months ago when my mentor, Gerald, retired."

"How funny that we went to the same school?"

"Well, it is the best."

"That it is."

Then comes the question I dread. "What about your family?"

Thankfully, the waitress appears with the wine. She uncorks the bottle and pours a little for Marlee to taste. She picks up the glass, swirls the liquid around, inhales, and then takes a sip. My eyes lock on her lips as they wrap around the glass, then I envision them wrapped around my cock and it sliding in and out of her delectable mouth. I'm now sporting an erection that's harder than this wooden table. Just when I think it can't get any more uncomfortable in my pants, she moans, "Ohh, my God, this Verdelho is divine."

"Yeah, it's a great vintage," the waitress replies, as she tops off our glasses. She and Marlee chat about the wines on the menu for a few moments, which gives me a chance to deflate my cock and compose myself. Never have I had a reaction like this to a woman before. I'm confused. I'm intrigued. I'm horny. But most of all, I'm excited to see where this will lead.

Marlee looks over at me when the waitress leaves. "Sorry about that."

"No, it's fine. It's nice to see you so passionate, even if it is about wine. Maybe you need to teach me a few things."

"I'd like that," she says, flipping her jet-black hair over her shoulder. She picks up her glass and lifts for a toast. "A toast, to new friendships and a newfound appreciation of wine."

Picking up my glass, I raise it toward hers. "I'll toast to that."

We clink our glasses gently, and with our eyes locked on one another we drink. The air around us suddenly becomes thick and heated. Everything around me fades away, all I see is Marlee and her wine. As we sip our wine silently, staring at one another, I decide I won't bed her tonight…I'll bide my time and make it perfect.

We finish the bottle of wine and I wave the waitress over to get the bill. Snatching the bill up, I wink at Marlee before handing my credit card over to pay. Once that's finalized, we stand up, exit the bar, and head to my car.

We are walking side by side, our pinkie fingers keep brushing and we are fighting the invisible—will we/won't we—hold hands but before any handholding happens we reach my car. A force beyond my control overtakes my body, I spin Marlee around, push her up against my car.

Grip her cheeks in my palms and I stare into her eyes before I slam my lips against hers.

She gasps in shock. For a few fleeting seconds she doesn't kiss me back, and I start to think I shouldn't have kissed her. I'm put at ease when she drapes her arms around my shoulders, pulls me closer to her, and begins to kiss me back. Her tongue seeks access to my mouth and I willingly accept. As soon as I slightly open, she slips her tongue inside. Closing my eyes, I lose myself in the moment. Nothing but this kiss matters right now.

This is the perfect first kiss.

All too soon, she breaks the connection and rests her forehead against mine.

"I'm sorry," I whisper.

"Don't be." She pauses, her tongue darts out and she licks her lip—I want to lick her lip—then she gently bites it. "Gage," she whispers. "I liked it. In fact," she breathes deeply, and quietly adds, "I'd like to do it again." Before I can protest, she places her lips gently against mine. She grips my cheeks and presses her lips harder against mine. This kiss is much softer but it's just as amazing as our first.

An urge I can't control overtakes my body, I thread my fingers into her hair. Digging my fingers into her scalp. The kiss turns from sweet and innocent to heated and rough in the blink of an eye. She wraps her arms around my shoulders and presses her entire body against mine. Your can't tell where I end and she begins. We become one. She moans into my mouth as she lifts her leg and wraps it around my thigh, pressing her pussy into my leg and gently grinding. We both groan and continue to kiss. Our hands roam each other's bodies. Nearby, a car's engine starts and that snaps us both back to reality. She drops her leg and we pull apart.

Marlee is leaning against my car. Her chest heaving. Her lips swollen. She lifts her hand and runs her finger over her lips. My eyes follow the motion before drifting up to her eyes. We stare intently at one another. She smiles shyly at me. "So, ummm…"

"Yeah." I reply, digging my hands into my pocket, suddenly it's awkward and uncomfortable. "I'll, umm, ahh, drop you home."

"Thanks," she replies.

Unlocking my car, I lean around her and open her door. She squeezes my hand and smiles at me, the awkwardness of the previous moments evaporate with that one touch. She climbs in and I close the door.

Walking around the front, I look through the window and watch her. I swear she mouths, 'What the hell,' and it brings a smile to my face. Opening my door, I climb in and look over to her. "So, where to?"

"I'm just round the corner from the store where we bumped into each other."

"Me too. I live in the Grove apartments." Her head snaps toward me and her mouth drops open. "What?" I question.

"I live across the road in the Grosvenor building."

"No way."

"Yes, way."

We both stare at one another grinning. Shaking my head, I laugh. "I can't believe you live so close. How long have you lived there?"

"I moved in just before I started my job. Prior to that, I was in the residence halls on Lincoln Avenue. It's so nice to have my own space. Don't get me wrong, I loved living with Sheridan, but it's nice to be able to do what I want when I want. You know?"

"Yeah, I do. I've lived here for as long as I can remember." My mind drifts to that moment. I'd just turned eighteen and I was finally getting away from Dad. He didn't give two shits about me leaving, to be honest; he probably didn't even notice I wasn't there. Not until the recycling was overflowing with empties. I was ever so thankful to finally have access to the life insurance that Ma left for me. It was a pretty hefty amount, which allowed me to buy my penthouse apartment and splurge on my car. Not enough for my dream car of an Aston Martin Vanquish, but I can always dream…and drool.

"It's such a great area to live in," Marlee says, bringing me back to the present.

"It sure is."

We fall silent as I drive us home. Pulling into the garage under my building, I park in my spot and we walk over to the elevators. I press the button for ground when we step in. When they open to the lobby, I place my hand on her lower back and escort her outside and across the road.

We awkwardly stand at the steps to her building, staring at one another.

"Thank for you for the drink."

"You're welcome. Maybe next time, we can grab something to eat too." *What the hell? I'm asking her out again?*

"I'd like that," she quietly discloses, brushing a wayward stand of hair behind her ear.

She steps toward me, putting her hands on my chest and places her lips on my cheek. "Good night, Gage," she whispers, before turning away from me and walking up the stairs to her building. Watching her walk up the stairs, I smile.

She enters the building and turns to look back at me. She offers a wave as the door closes. I stand watching until she steps into the elevator and out of sight.

Turning around, I walk back across the road and enter my building. As I wait for the elevator, my mind flits back to Marlee and the interesting night we just had together. This woman intrigues me like no other has before, and if I'm honest, I really want to get to know her on a deeper level. The elevator doors open and as I step in, I think to myself, *Damn you, Kasey Wellson, for being right.*

CHAPTER 6

Slamming back my drink, I pour another. Loosening my tie, I walk over to my couch and sit down. Flicking the television on, I switch to *SportsCenter*. After finishing my drink, I place my tumbler in the sink and walk into my bedroom.

Stripping off, I climb into the shower. Hoping the water will ease my turmoil over Marlee. As I soap myself up, my hand drifts to my cock. It hardens beneath my touch. Gripping the base, I gently stroke. Leaning one arm against the tiles, I rest my forehead on my forearm and close my eyes, picturing Marlee's delicate fingers in place of mine. My strokes become faster and faster. My breathing hurried. My balls tighten and I explode with a grunt into my hand, cum spraying the wall. I feel relieved but also dirty at the same time.

How can I use someone as sweet and angelic as Marlee in this depraved and filthy way? Shaking my head, I step under the water and wash away the dirtiness of what I just did. *How can something feel so good but so dirty at the same time?*

Climbing out, I dry off and slip on a pair of Batman boxers before I brush my teeth. Switching off all the lights, I then fall into bed. Lying down, I stare at the ceiling. Sleep eludes me as my mind keeps playing that kiss with Marlee over and over in my head.

The feel of her soft lips against mine.

The sound she made when I deepened the kiss.

The warmth of her body pressed against mine.

Her hands running up my back.

Fuck! I'm hard again, but this time I think of fat naked ladies and my cock instantly deflates, even though Marlee is still at the forefront of my imagination. It's like she's possessed my mind, she's all I can think about. If I'm like this after one kiss and one tug, what will I be like after I fuck her?

Eventually I drift off to sleep, and the last thing I remember is seeing a vision of Marlee smiling and laughing, with not a care in the world.

The next morning, I walk into the office with a pep in my step. I feel light and free, for the first time in years, and it's all to do with Marlee. Stepping out of the elevator, I pause midstep and smile, when I see Marlee and Chelle walking past reception.

Racing to my office, I dump my briefcase and make a beeline for Chelle's office.

Walking in without knocking I say, "Morning, ladies," interrupting Marlee as she chats with Chelle.

She looks over her shoulder at me and says, "Morning." While I get a head nod from Chelle.

Marlee ignores my presence and continues to talk to Chelle, effectively dismissing me. Her brush-off pisses me off. Standing in the doorway, I look between the two of them. They are engrossed in their conversation and continue to ignore me. Neither of them makes any move to include me in their discussion. Shaking my head, I turn on my heel and storm back to my office. Completely pissed off they ignored me; in particular that Marlee shunned me.

Marching back to my office, I slam my office door, sit down at my desk, and throw myself into work. Well, I try to work but I keep thinking about being rejected just now. Clearly, she felt nothing after our kiss last night, the way she just ignored me really pisses me off. I'd expect that from Chelle, but not Marlee.

Two hours later, my back is aching from pouring over this report. Grabbing my coffee mug, I walk toward to kitchen for another coffee. When I walk in, Marlee is at the coffee machine. When she see's it's me, her face lights up like a Christmas tree.

"Hey, Gage," she sweetly says. "How's your morning? Chelle and I have been super busy and just about have everything worked out for the toy drive." Her reaction right now is confusing to me. Not two hours ago she completely ignored me, well not completely, she did say morning. But now it seems like I'm the center of attention, and she continues to chat away. I'm staring at her, I see her lips moving but I have no fucking clue what she just said. My eyes are locked on her lips, lips that twelve hours ago were locked with mine…and I really want them locked on mine again.

"Gage," she says, raising her voice to get my attention.

"Sorry, what was that?"

"I said did you want to grab lunch?"

"No," I tersely reply.

Her face deflates. "Ohh, okay. Well, have a great day." She pushes past me, leaving the coffee she was making half-made.

"Fuck!" I mumble, turning around I chase after her, but by time I make it to reception, the elevator doors are closing. Pinching the bridge of my nose, I sigh and walk back to my office, forgetting all about my coffee and pissed at myself for being so rude to Marlee…and internally laughing at myself as to why I care. She's just a chick after all, but she's a smoking hot chick that I can't stop thinking about, and that pisses me off. I don't constantly think about chicks. But there is something about Marlee Adams that makes me care. Something that makes me want more.

CHAPTER 7

She looks at me, and sharply hisses, "Do you even need to ask?"

Before I can answer, the elevator doors open and she races toward Chelle's office. I'm left standing in the elevator, stunned and confused. The doors begin to close, and I put my hand up to stop them. Walking into reception, Stacey glares at me before answering the phone. *What the fuck did I do to her?* I think to myself as I walk toward my office.

Later that day, I'm coming out of the kitchen when the new intern sees me. He quickly turns on his heel, does a one-eighty before smacking into the conference room door. After stumbling, he quickly runs away from me. I've never even spoke to the guy, yet he scurries away from me quicker than a fat kid can inhale an ice-cream cone. To be honest, it was funny to see so I laughed, but it's also disconcerting at the same time.

Why are people running from me?

Why is everyone pissed at me?

What the fuck have I done?

By time Friday rolls around, I'm angry with the world, living up to my name of the Christmas Grinch. Anything and everything pisses me, people are even hiding from me now. My question is answered mid-morning Friday when Kasey storms into my office. She slams the door behind her, and I can tell from the expression on her face that she's pissed off.

"To what do I owe the pleasure, Ms. Wellson, soon to be Mrs. Holmes?"

"Don't 'to what do I owe the pleasure' bullshit me, Grainger, why did you do it?"

"Huh?" I ask, genuinely confused, because apart from being snarky with everyone, I haven't specifically done anything wrong…I don't think.

"Marlee," she spits out, crossing her arms. Pushing her boobs up and my eyes drift to them—hey, I'm a man, give me a break. She glowers at me. "Well?"

"Well, what?" I'm really confused now, her boobs have distracted me and I forgot what she just said. She slams her palms on my desk and snaps, "Marlee!"

I hear her that time and with that one word, I'm speechless…and still confused. "What about Marlee? I haven't seen or spoken to her since Wednesday morning during a really uncomfortable elevator trip."

"Exactly," she says, hands on her hips and her eyes throwing daggers at me.

"I have no idea what you are getting at."

"Gage, I told you not to mess with her."

"I haven't. On Monday night we had a drink. Then we kissed. And then she ignored me. End of story."

"Yeah, because after you kissed her, you slept with that skanky ho in accounting."

Now I'm even more confused. "Huh?"

"On Tuesday, Crissy told Halle, who told Beth, Amanda and Shez, who then spilled to Chelle, Marlee, and me that on Monday night you slept with Mandy in accounting."

"What?"

"Gage, I told you not to fuck around with Marlee, and within the first few days you fuck it all up. I'm—"

"Stop," I growl, lifting my hand up for emphasis. "I haven't slept with anyone this week. Even if I had: A. It's none of your business if I did, and B. My dick will never go anywhere near Mandy and her vagina. Even I have standards. And C. Apart from a kiss, I haven't done anything to Marlee."

"But..."

"Is that why Marlee is angry with me? And why everyone is steering clear of me and giving me the evil eye?"

"So, you didn't sleep with Mandy?"

"Fuck no. Not for a billion trillion dollars would I sleep with her." That's when I register why Marlee is upset. "Hang on, why is Marlee upset? She dismissed me Tuesday morning. Then we had an awkward elevator ride Wednesday morning."

"Okay, let me dumb it down for you. Tuesday, she ignored you as she was here working. Gage, the world doesn't revolve around you and your dick. On Wednesday, she ignored you because she found out Tuesday afternoon that you fucked someone else hours after kissing her. Gage, she likes, well, liked you, but when she's here, she's working. You really are dim sometimes. Marlee wants to make a good impression at Chicago Hopes. If your ego got bruised 'cause she chose work over chatting with you, then you deserve to be shunned by everyone…even if it is for the wrong reason." She pauses. "Now, how are you going to fix this? But before you do, elaborate on this kiss."

"You are more of a gossip than Halle and Crissy combined. I'm not talking about my kiss with Marlee. It's none of your business." Leaning my elbows on my desk, I rub my temples. Looking up at Kasey I ask, "How upset is she?"

"She's crushed. That must have been some kiss. Gage, when she heard about Mandy, she deflated instantly. She was hurt deeply. You need to fix this."

"How do I do that?"

She shrugs her shoulders. "No idea, but I know where she'll be tonight. Maybe you could pop by and smooth things over."

"I'll give it a go. Where and when?"

"We are meeting at Branson and Kody's new bar, Bin 501." I laugh when I hear this. "What's so funny?"

"That's where we had drinks. Our kiss happened in the parking lot."

"So romantic, Gage, in the parking lot. But it's also perfect, it can be the place where you fix this."

"What time?"

"We are heading there from here. Be you usual asshole self until five, then when we leave here, give us an hour or so to unwind, AND then swoop in and fix this with Marlee, because she is the best thing to come into your life." She pauses and adds, "And you both deserve to be happy, Gage."

Nodding my head, my mind flits to Marlee. No wonder she's pissed at me. *Fucking, Mandy*. When I look up, I see Kasey is no longer in my office. I laugh that she would leave without saying goodbye, but then again, that's Kase.

For the rest of the afternoon, I try to work on this report, but my mind keeps drifting to Marlee and what I'm going to do to fix this. *What is this woman doing to me? I don't care about their feelings, I don't care about them at all... until now, until Marlee.*

Finally, 5:45 p.m. rolls around, shutting off my Mac, I grab my stuff and leave. Walking to my car many different scenarios of what will happen when I arrive at Bin 501 run through my mind. They range from a slap, her throwing herself at me, and my biggest fear, her blowing me off and ignoring me. That last scenario scares me the most. Never has a woman held my attention like Marlee has, I want more...that both thrills and terrifies me.

Parking my car in the same spot as the last time I was here, I take that as a good sign. Walking across the parking lot, my nerves kick in. With sweaty palms, I take a deep breath and swing the door open. Stepping inside, I look up and freeze. My mouth drops open and my heart stops beating.

CHAPTER 8

MY EYES ARE LOCKED ON MARLEE, HER HEAD IS THROWN back and she's laughing. Tonight, she looks sensational, she's always stunning but this evening she is exceptionally gorgeous. She's wearing a sexy, little black halter number that hugs her curves and showcases her ohh-so-sexy legs and ass. Her feet are encased in a pair of super high heels and they only accentuate the sexiness of her lower half. She leans her elbows on the high-top table, pushing her breasts together...breasts I want to lose myself in. The women around her are pretty, but none of them hold a candle to my Marlee...yes, MY Marlee.

Kasey notices me and smiles, nodding to Marlee, she raises her eyebrows in a 'go get em', tiger' kind of way.

Putting one foot in front of the other, I make my way over to the group just as Kasey's fiancé, Kody, comes over to join them. Kase stands up and he kisses her passionately. I watch the two of them together, and for the first time in my life, I want that. I want what they have. Unconditional love and eyes only for one another. My gaze drifts to Marlee and I'm happy to see that she's staring at me. I smile at her but when I do, she immediately looks away. My hearts deflates a little at this, but I know that I need to set her straight in regard to Mandy. *Fucking, Mandy.*

Needing liquid courage, I head toward the bar.

"What can I get you?" the bartender asks.

"Two glasses of ver-something-o, please?"

He laughs at me, "Verdelho?"

"That's the one."

"Coming right up."

With our drinks in hand, I walk back to the group. I'm just about to approach Marlee when Mandy stops me. "Is one of them for me?" she purrs.

"No," I snap in reply. My voice louder than I expected and everyone from work turns to look at us. Marlee's face drops when she sees who I'm chatting with. Mandy, rests her hand on my arm and I flinch at the contact. "Stop, Mandy. There is nothing between us and there never will be. And I don't appreciate you spreading false rumors around about me." My eyes are locked on Marlee's as I say this.

"But—"

"No, no buts, Mandy." I look back at her and stare daggers at her. "Never. Going. To. Happen." I pause between each word for emphasis. Mandy huffs and stalks off. Kasey gives me a thumbs-up. Nodding, I smile back at her and turn my attention back to Marlee and take the final few steps so I'm standing in front of her.

"Hey there," I quietly say, greeting her how she greeted me in the grocery store the other day.

"Hi," she shyly replies in return as I place one of the wine glasses on the table in front of her. My heart is beating a million miles a minute, suddenly I'm nervous. "I got you a glass of vermelho."

She looks up at me confused, her eyebrows scrunch in confusion. "Verdelho?"

"Yeah, that's what I said," I reply, my eyes locked on hers.

She shakes her head. "Nope. Pretty sure you just said vermelho." She's smirking at me. "Seems there's a lot I need to teach you about wine, Gage Grainger."

Hearing her say my name stirs something inside of me and without thinking or missing a beat, I hesitantly ask, "How about you teach me over dinner then?"

Everything around me fades away.

The noise of the bar silences around me.

I'm focused on Marlee, and Marlee only.

She's focused on me in return.

Our eyes are fused to one another.

We stare intently at each other.

She swallows deeply.

I swallow deeply.

She smiles.

I smile.

Quietly she finally murmurs, "I'd like that."

From the other end of the table, I hear Kasey loudly whisper, "Yes." And from the corner of my eye, I see her fist pump the air triumphantly.

"Great. Awesome," I goofily say in reply. *What is this woman doing to me?* I once again say to myself, as I take the empty seat beside her, placing my glass on the table next to hers.

Leaning back in my chair, I rest my arm across the back of her chair and pick up my glass. "A toast. To learning more about wine…and you."

She blushes when I add the 'and you' part but she picks up her glass. "I'll drink to that," she says, as she gently taps her glass against mine. She brings the glass to her lips, my eyes watch intently as she takes a sip. She swallows before her tongue darts out to lick her bottom lip, gently biting it.

Leaning into her, I run my nose up to her ear and whisper, "I'd really like to lick and bite that lip."

Her eyes snap to mine, and she whispers, "I'd really like you to bite my lip," lowering her voice she sexily murmurs, "and lick other things."

Bending forward, I softly place my lips against hers for a kiss. Before I pull back, I gently nip and tug on her bottom lip. Pulling back, I notice her neck and cheeks are pink, aroused pink. Her breathing is labored. Her eyes full of lust and desire. Over her shoulder, I notice everyone at the table is staring at us; mouths open in shock.

Marlee notices where I'm looking and turns her head to see what I'm staring at. "What?" she asks.

"That was hot," Chelle says. "If I wasn't already knocked up, that would totally do it."

Marlee drops her gaze and stares at her lap, I find myself grinning. Leaning into her again, I ask, "Do you want to get out of here? Go somewhere, just the two of us?"

She looks up at me. She doesn't say anything for what feels like a million years, but in reality, it was only a few seconds. "I'd like that."

We quickly finish our drinks, stand up to leave, and say our goodbyes. Linking my fingers with hers, we walk out of the bar for a night that, hopefully, will be the beginning of something beautiful.

CHAPTER 9

WE OPEN THE DOOR AND STEP OUTSIDE, SNOW HAS STARTED TO fall again. The air is chilly yet heated at the same time. The connection between us is palpable. Marlee drops my hand and slips on her coat. Rather than putting my coat on, I take the time to check her out. *Fuck, she is gorgeous!* Never have I seen a more stunning woman. "You really are beautiful, Marlee," I say to her. Brushing a strand of her ink black hair behind her ear, I graze the tips of my finger along her chin, before cupping her cheek. Gently I rub my thumb just under her ear. We both stare at one another for a few moments. Even with the snow falling, the air around us is warm and thick with arousal.

We step forward at the same time. Our lips crash

together. Our tongues flick and dance and slide together. Our hands roam and squeeze and explore.

It's carnal.

It's heated.

It's raw.

It's definitely not suitable for public, but we are both lost in the moment with not a care in the world. The moment is broken when the door behind us opens. We jump and quickly pull apart, her cheeks darken with embarrassment. I'm trying to hold back a laugh, as soon as the couple steps past us; I grab her hand and drag her toward my car. When we reach the passenger side, I press her against the door and slam my lips against hers.

A moment of déjà vu occurs, but I brush it aside and continue to assault Marlee's mouth with my tongue.

We pull apart, both of us breathing heavily.

I stare at her.

She stares at me.

"Take me home," she breathlessly whispers.

"With pleasure," I roughly growl.

Unlocking my car, I open the door for her and wait for her to slide into her seat. With a grin on my face, I quickly round the hood, climb into the driver's seat, and speed back to my place.

Pulling into my parking spot, Marlee is out of the car before I even have my belt off. She waits for me by the hood, her chest heaving, her eyes full of desire and need. My cock is hard as a rock; painfully pressing against my zipper. Stalking toward her, I grip her cheeks and slam my lips against hers. She grips my shoulders and returns the kiss. Pulling back, she pants, "Upstairs. Now." Tugging on my hand, she drags us toward to elevators.

She pushes the button and the doors immediately open. *That never happens*, I think to myself as we climb in and press the button for my floor. As soon as the doors close, Marlee pounces. She pushes me against the sidewall and covers my mouth with hers. She runs her hand down my chest and grips me through my dress pants. I moan into her mouth as she squeezes me harder. Gripping her wrist, I hold her firmly. "Marl, if you keep that up, I'm going to come in my pants in this elevator."

She giggles and pulls her hand away and steps back.

We stare at one another as the doors begin to close—I hadn't even realized we had arrived at my floor. Lifting my hand, I stop the doors closing and we both step out.

Marlee looks up and down the corridor, unsure of which way to go. Grabbing her hand, I pull her down the hall toward my door at the end. Digging into my pocket, I pull my keys out. My movements are thwarted as Marlee wraps her arms around me from behind. She's already unbuttoning my shirt, running her palms along my abs, and right in this moment, I'm wishing I'd hit the gym.

She nibbles my neck just below my ear, and whispers, "Hurry the fuck up, Grainger, or I'm going to mount you in the hallway here and give your neighbor a show."

Turning my head, I glare at her and growl, "Not fucking happening, woman." She giggles and it sends shock waves straight to my already straining cock.

Quickly, I slip the key into the chamber, turn, unlock, and shove the door open. Grabbing her hand, I pull her into my apartment. Kicking the door shut with my foot, I spin her around, slamming her against the door. Her head snaps back and hits the wood. "Ow," she says, as she rubs the back of her head.

"Shit, sorry," I apologize, but before I can assess if she's okay, she spins us around so my back is now against the door. She grips me though my pants and licks her lips. She stares intently at me as her nimble fingers undo my belt, pop the button, and lower my zipper. She pushes her hand in and around to my ass, squeezing my ass cheeks before shimmying my briefs and pants down my legs. She lowers to her knees and licks her lips. Her eyes are locked on mine, as her tongue darts out and she gently grazes her tongue over the tip. Her touch is featherlight, but it sends lightning bolts through my body and I groan in pleasure.

She opens her mouth and wraps her lips around my shaft, I almost come there and then. Her sexy hot mouth wrapped around my cock is pure bliss. It's fucking heaven. She bobs her head and slides my cock in and out of her mouth, I lose all motor function. I groan and garble incoherent words. Never has a blowjob felt so good before. She reaches up and cups my balls, massaging the pleasure spot that immediately sets me off, and I come without warning. She sucks every last drop from me.

She removes her mouth from my cock, lifts her finger, and sexily wipes a spill. With her eyes on me, she slips her finger into her mouth and sucks. "MMMMM," she murmurs as I slide down the door. My ass hits the cold tiles but I'm too wiped to care. *Best fucking blowjob of my life.* With a smile on my face, I lean back into the door and let out a contented sigh.

Marlee shimmies forward and straddles my lap. She rests her palms on my chest and grins when she feels how fast my heart is beating. Removing her hands, she grips the hem of her dress and lifts it over her head. My heart stops beating at the stunning sight before me. She's wearing the sexiest strapless bra I have ever seen. It's sheer and showcases her cleavage perfectly.

My hand lifts on their own accord and I cup her plump mounds. They fit in my palms perfectly, I gently squeeze, garnering a sexy little moan from her. Leaning forward, I pull the cup of her bra down and lower my mouth. My tongue darts out and swirls around the tip before I suck her nipple, forming a perfect stiff peak. With my thumb and fingertip, I pinch and roll her nipple between my fingers. She throws her head back, moans, and begins to grind herself on my legs.

She lifts her head and stares directly at me. Reaching behind her back, she unclasps her bra and drops it onto the tiled floor beside us. With a smile, I mash my face between her breasts. Nipping and licking across her skin. As I massage one breast, I suck on the other before licking across her chest, repeating the process again and again. Kissing my way up her chest, and along her chin, I reach her lips. Gently placing my lips against hers, we kiss. It's slow. It's sensual. It's soft. It's full of passion but it quickly turns heated and carnal.

Running my palms down her side, I skim my finger along the top of her panties before cupping her mound. The material is soaked with her arousal. "You're so wet," I murmur into our kiss, as I continue to stroke up and down her slit; she moans in reply as I push the material aside and slip a finger into her sex. She groans into the kiss as I pump my finger in and out. Slipping in a second finger, she moans my name and never has my name sounded so erotic. I press my thumb down on her clit, her head flies back, and she explodes around my fingers, screaming my name as her orgasm unleashes.

Leaning forward she rests her forehead on my shoulder as I remove my fingers. She sits back and watches as I bring my fingers to my mouth and lick them clean. Her cheeks are a shade that I like to call orgasmic pink, her chest is heaving. She licks her bottom lip and quietly whispers, "Fuck me, Gage."

She doesn't need to ask me twice.

My cock is once again rock-hard. She slides her panties down her thighs and quickly slips them off. I reach into my pants, pull out my wallet, and grab a condom. She takes it from my fingers, tears it open with her teeth, and slides it down my cock. Lifting onto her knees, she rests her hands on my shoulders and with our eyes on one another, she slides down my shaft. When she's fully seated, she looks down and watches as she thrusts her hips sliding up and down my cock. My eyes track down her body and watch as her pussy clenches around me. Lifting my arms, I wrap them around her back for support as she increases her thrusts. She makes a moan in the back of her throat and I know she's close. I'm close too but I will myself not to come until she has. Sliding my hand between us, I press on her clit, and with a guttural cry, she clenches my cock tighter causing us to come together. We moan and groan as pleasure rockets throughout our bodies.

We both still, she collapses into my shoulder and I hug her closer to me. We are both panting like we've just run a marathon. She raises her head and with a smile that lights up her face, she whispers, "Wow."

"You ain't see nothing yet, baby," I pant in reply. She giggles and snuggles into my chest farther. Her breath warming my already heated skin. With my arms around her lower back, I stand up. She wraps her legs around my waist and drapes her arms over my shoulders as I toe off my shoes and kick off my pants. Walking us into my apartment, I step through the living room, into my bedroom, and head for the shower. Leaning in, I turn it on and step back. Once the water is warm, I step in. Marlee is still in my arms and when the warm water hits us, we both sigh in pleasure. Our bodies tense and exhausted after our doorway fuck.

She lowers herself down, squirts some of my bodywash into her hands and begins to soap me up. Her hands glide over my body and my cock starts to stir again. I've got good stamina, but never like this before. Marlee does things to me like no one ever has. When she starts to soap herself up, I groan and she smirks. Watching her hands rub over her breasts and between her legs is so sexy. "Marlee, that is the sexiest thing I have ever seen."

She looks at me and with a smirk, and huskily says, "What? This?" She lifts her leg and places her foot on the shower bench, slides her hand down her stomach, and runs her finger down her slit and slips it between her lips. She moans. I groan. The air around us, hot and steamy, thick with desire and need.

My hand grips my cock. Our eyes are fused to one another while our fingers and hands pleasure ourselves. I come quickly, embarrassingly quickly, but when you have a naked, wet Marlee fingering herself, you would too. She comes with a quiet moan and then lifts her hand to my lips for me to lick her juices. She slides her finger past my lips. Wrapping my lips around her digit, I suck and lick it clean.

She steps toward me and presses her lips and body hard against mine. Her tongue seeks access to my mouth and I willingly open and let her in. We kiss and fondle one another until the water runs cold. Stepping out, we dry ourselves. Our eyes steadfastly locked on one another.

Once dry, I stretch out my hand. She places hers in mine and I walk us into my bedroom. Pulling back the covers, I climb in and she climbs in beside me. Lying on my back, she snuggles into my side, throwing her leg over mine. We cuddle one another and drift off to sleep. Well fucked and blissfully happy.

CHAPTER 10

THE NEXT MORNING, I WAKE BEFORE MARLEE. THE SHEET HAS slipped down and her perfectly pert nipple is begging for me to taste it. Rolling to my side, I lower my head and suck her nipple into my mouth as my hand slides down her side and between her legs. She spreads her legs slightly and I slide my fingers between her lips. She's already wet and ready for me. Slipping two fingers into her, she moans and grinds herself against my hand. Her body pulsating under my touch, instantly coming alive.

She runs her fingers through my hair and with her nipple in my mouth, I gaze up at her. She looks gorgeous first thing in the morning. With my hand still between her legs, I kiss and nip my way up to her mouth. Pressing my lips against hers, I slip a third finger in and she moans. My tongue assaults her mouth as my fingers pump in and out of her.

"Fuuuuuuuck!" she growls as her orgasm explodes. When her body shudders stop and she looks toward me, her eyes are hazy with lust.

"Good morning," I huskily greet, brushing a stand of hair off her forehead.

"Good morning indeed," she purrs, rolling to her side, resting her head in her palm. The look on her face is indescribable, she looks great in my bed and I want to keep her here for as long as possible. She reaches out and runs her finger just above my eyebrow, my skin buzzing from her touch. Leaning forward, she places her lips against mine for a gentle morning kiss.

The grumbling of her stomach breaks the moment and we both laugh. My stomach soon rumbles in response. "Guess we both are hungry?" I say.

"Mmmhmpf," she replies, as she wraps her hand around my cock. With a squeeze, she adds, "I think I'll dine in." Before I can react, she scoots down the bed and wraps her lips around me. Gripping the base, she slides my cock in and out of her mouth. Applying the right amount of pressure, mixed with a gentle scraping of her teeth. Without warning, my cock jerks and I come. Just like last night, she sucks every last drop, and as she lies back next to me, she licks her lips.

"You and your sexy as fuck mouth will be the death of me, woman."

She shrugs her shoulders nonchalantly and gives me the sexiest grin I have ever seen. "If you want to keep my sexy ass happy, you better feed me coffee so I can recharge for round two."

"Fuck," I groan, this woman is perfect. "You had me at ass." Climbing out of bed, I walk to the stool at the end of my bed and slip on a pair of sweats that sit low on my hips. When I turn around, Marlee is staring at me. Intently. I feel it deep in my bones. "If you keep looking at me like that, coffee and breakfast will be delayed and we'll jump right to round two."

"That also works," she says, throwing the sheet off before lying back on the bed. She spreads her legs, giving me a perfect view of her pussy. She skims her finger around her nipple, it instantly puckers...much like my cock right now. Jumping onto the bed, I lower myself down, cocooning her underneath me. I suck on the nipple she was just teasing me with. Lifting my head, I stare down at her. Her eyes are a vivid blue gray in the morning light. "You, my lil' minx, are going to have to wait." I place a kiss on the tip of her nose and climb off of her. "Help yourself to a shirt it my closet," I invite, as I hop off and walk out of my bedroom to start breakfast.

"Asshole," I hear her mumble.

"I heard that," I shout as I exit the bedroom.

"You were meant to," she playfully replies.

With a grin on my face, I head into the kitchen and am happy to see that there is a pot of coffee brewed and waiting. Grabbing two cups, I place them on the counter and fill them up. I've just placed the pot back on the warmer when Marlee walks out in one of my U. Of I. tees...and she looks much better than I do in it.

"Fuck me," I mumble.

"We could be, but you chose coffee over this." She

flicks her hand up and down her body as she takes a seat on the barstool across from me.

Shaking my head, I grab the creamer from the fridge and slide it and a mug across to Marlee. She looks shocked. "You know I take creamer?"

"I know lots about you, Marlee Adams."

"Is that so, Gage Grainger?"

Nodding my head, I lift my mug to my mouth and take a sip of coffee.

"Okay then, what else do you know about me?"

"Everything," I cockily say.

"Name three things about me and it can't be about coffee," she challenges.

Grabbing my cup, I round the kitchen island and take the stool next to her. "Okay. You like white wine with fancy schmanzy names."

"Okay, I'll give you that. And two?"

"You live across the road from me."

"That's two. And the third?"

"You aren't wearing any panties right now, and I bet, from me doing this…" I slide my finger across her chin, down her neck and over her—my—shirt, grazing her breast with my pinkie as I trail my finger down her stomach and circle just above her mound, "…you are wet and aching for me."

She swallows deeply and clenches her thighs together. "Nope," she breathlessly denies.

"Prove it," I challenge her back.

"Damn it!" she huffs, spinning on her stool to face me. She spreads her legs, and I trace my finger between her thighs.

"Yep, just as I suspected. Wet for me."

Hopping off my stool, I spin her around so her back leans against the counter. Dropping to my knees, I spread her legs wide open and lean forward. I breathe in her scent and moan. My tongue darts out and I lick up her lips, flicking her clit with my tongue. She grips my head and pushes me deeper between her thighs. I suck and lap at her slit. When I slide a finger into her channel, she rocks and moans. Tapping her leg, she lifts it over my shoulder, giving me more room to pleasure her. My fingers thrusts in and out, curling to reach that magic spot deep inside. When I suck on her clit, she nearly jumps off the chair. Her orgasm hits out of nowhere and she screams my name as she soaks my fingers and face.

Pulling back, I look up at her and lick my lips. "Breakfast of champions," I tease.

She smacks my head. "That's gross."

"You loved it."

"Yeah, but that's different."

"I beg to differ." Rising to my feet, I sit back on the stool next to her. "So, what shall we do today?"

"Ummm," she pauses, "I didn't think you'd want me hanging around."

"Marlee," I say, reaching over to grab her hand. "I want to get to know you. You have this effect on me that I can't explain, and I want to keep feeling like this. I haven't been this happy since…" I drift off when I realize that the last time I was this happy, Ma was still alive.

"Happy since when?" she asks.

Looking at her, I realize that she genuinely wants to know. "Not since Ma was alive," I sadly say.

"I'm sorry, Gage. I couldn't imagine losing my mom." She jumps up. "I have the perfect idea. I'm going to run across the road and change. Meet me out front in twenty minutes." She grabs her dress from the entryway and skips into my bedroom. A few minutes later, she walks out in her dress from last night. She walks over to me and kisses me on the lips. "Twenty minutes." She squeezes my forearm, turns, heads to the door, and exits my apartment. I sit and stare at the door, wondering what just happened, but also excited for the day ahead.

Twenty minutes later, I'm waiting out front. I'm staring at her building and don't notice a black pimped-out Jeep pull up. A beeping horn snaps my attention to the car, and I look over and see a smiling Marlee staring back at me. She rolls down the window. "Jump in and let's go."

CHAPTER II

"Nope," she says. "But afterward we can do something of your choosing."

"Really? Anything?"

She nods her head, bites her lip, leans in, and sexily whispers, "I've got an idea on what we can do, but it's not suitable since we are in public."

"How about we just get right to that event instead?"

"Nope, you have to wait, 'cause we are here."

Looking around, I see we are in Millennium Park. "Are we going ice-skating?" She nods her head. "I haven't skated in years."

"Don't worry, I'll help you. I might even go for a

sneaky grab here and there too." She winks at me and drags me toward the ice rink.

An hour later, I'm exhausted. I forgot how much energy you need to ice-skate. Marlee is a pro, she looks angelic skating around. Me? I looked like a newborn calf trying to walk for the first time—not graceful at all. But seeing Marlee laugh at my ice-skating plight was totally worth the humiliation.

We change back into our shoes and grab a cup of hot cocoa. Linking hands, we get our hot chocolate to go and decide to take a walk around the park. We chat and get to know each other more. I discover that she's an only child, her parents are high school sweethearts and have been together since they were seventeen. She loves white wine, especially Verdelho. Ben and Jerry's Chocolate Chip Cookie Dough is her go to ice-cream flavor, and she's not a fan of baths.

I tell her that I too am an only child. I'm a whiskey drinker. Not particular on a specific ice-cream flavor, and I also don't really like baths, but I do love a hot tub…especially on a cold winter's evening. And I invite her over tonight to join me in mine, as I just so happen to have one on my patio. I manage to steer clear of my parents, and for now, she doesn't push the subject.

That's one of the things I love about Marlee, she listens but she also picks up on what I don't say. She understands me on a level that no one ever before has.

We are walking back to the car when she does ask, "Gage, what happened to your parents? You've mentioned that your mom has passed."

"I lost them one Christmas when I was ten years old." I

don't elaborate that Dad is still alive but to me, when Ma died, I lost him too.

"Ohh, Gage. I'm so sorry. No wonder you hate Christmas." She squeezes my hand and then wraps her arm around my waist, snuggling in. "Tell me about your mom."

"She was the best mom there ever was. She'd do anything and everything for you. She used to bake hundreds of cookies for the church each Christmas, that's why I donate to the toy drive. I can't bake for shit, but me assisting keeps her memory alive." Pausing, I look up at the sky and grin. "She also taught me to predict when it would snow." Placing my finger under her chin, I lift so we are both looking up at the sky.

Together we both say, "It's going to snow again tonight."

We look back at each other. Both of us sporting grins. Lifting my hand, I run my finger down her cheek. The air around us heats and thickens, even though the outside temperature is near freezing. Stepping to her, I wrap my arm around her waist, pull her to me and lower my lips to hers for a soft and sensual kiss. Breaking the kiss, I pull back and gaze into her eyes. "You are exquisite, Marlee Adams. What did I ever do to have you fall into my life?"

"I don't know, Gage, but I'm glad we crashed into each other and that you groped my ass."

"I didn't grope, I saved you from certain death."

"My hero," she sarcastically replies, clutching her chest. "Now take me home and let me show you my thanks."

"Best idea ever."

Half an hour later, we are back at my place and we

show our thanks and appreciation of each other, all night long.

With a pep in my step, I walk through the food court on Monday morning, and for the first time in twenty years, the Christmas music doesn't grate on my nerves. I even find myself singing in my head when "Winter Wonderland" comes on. With a smile on my face, I step into the elevator and head up to WFOX-FM. The elevator doors open and I find Kasey and Kody in the reception area laughing.

"Morning, Buttercup," I say to Kase and earn myself a glare. Looking to Kody, I singsong "Morning." Yes, I singsong. *What the fuck is happening to me?*

"You're chipper for a Monday morning, Grainger," Kasey teases.

"Kace, leave him alone." Kody nudges her. "He's in love," he states matter-of-factly to us both. "Don't you remember what those first days of love are like? You smile like a loon. You are happy and carefree. Everything makes you grin, you even physically help out with the Christmas drive, even though you are known as the office Grinch."

Pausing, my mouth drops open when he says this and I stare at him. Am I in love with Marlee? No, I'm not, but the more I think about it, I think he's right. I am falling for her, but I don't do love. Love and happily ever afters have never been on my radar, but now that it's out there, I think he might be right. "I'm not a Grinch...or in love," I say without any conviction at all.

The two of them stare intently at me. Kasey walks over

to me and rests her palm on my arm. "Gage, are you in love with Marlee?"

CHAPTER 12

Staring at them, my heart begins to race erratically. "I…I…I'm not sure. I know she's the first person I think of when I wake up. She's on my mind all day. She's my last thought before I drift off to sleep. Hell, I even dream about her."

"Gage, that's love." Kasey happily replies, her face lit up with a smile.

"But—"

"No buts, you are in love with Marlee, and I for one am super happy for you. You deserve this."

"But, I don't now how to be in love. I'm not the guy who falls in love. I'm the—"

"Dude," Kody interrupts me. "There is no rhyme or

reason when it comes to love. It happens when you least expect it. It happens with a person that never in your wildest dream you think it would. No one can control love, just go with it. Everyone deserves love, Gage, even a Grinch like you."

"I'm not a Grinch. I just don't particularly like the festive season."

"Grinch," Kasey coughs, with a grin and laughs. "Gage, that is the definition of a Grinch, but this year there's a difference, you are a Grinch in love." she turns to Kody and I see love written all over her face, and I wonder if that's what I look like. "All right, fiancé, you need to go so I can get some work done."

He steps over to her, wraps his arms around her waist, and lowers his lips to hers. The kiss between them is soft but so full of love at the same time. He pulls back, places a kiss on the tip of her nose, and turns to the elevators. The doors open and he steps in, Kasey waves to him as the doors close. She turns to me, her cheeks are rosy and her eyes ablaze with lust. "Gage, I'm happy that you are finally opening up to someone. Marlee is a lucky gal."

She turns and walks down the hall toward her office. I stand in reception and watch her walk away, and I think about what they said. If I'm honest with myself, they are right. I **AM** falling in love with Marlee and I don't know what to do about it, this is new territory for me.

Shaking my head, I make my way to my office and get to it. This time of year is always busy with everyone wanting prime-time marketing spots, and the only good thing about it is how quickly the days fly by.

Marlee texted me just after lunch and said she'd come over tonight. She's going to bring Chinese and beer. We will have a quiet night in before I take her to bed, unwrap her, and make sweet, sweet love all night long. *Man, I'm turning into a lovesick sap.*

The day flies by and before I know it, it's time to head home. I'm in a bit of a mood as Dad called me again, but I sent it to voicemail. Being the gutless person that I am concerning him, I've yet to listen to his message.

As soon as I arrive home, I jump in the shower and let the hot water pound my muscles and wash away all the unease. I've just slipped into my lounge pants when there's a knock at the door. Walking over, I open the door and see a cheerfully happy Marlee. She has a Santa hat on her head, and she's wearing denim jeans that look like they are painted on and a black sweater. In her hands is a brown paper bag that smells amazing, a six-pack of beer, and a super big smile that lights up her entire face, which sets my heart racing.

Without saying anything, I step toward her, wrap my arms around her waist, pull her to me, and press my lips against hers. She slides her tongue into my mouth and what started as a gentle kiss quickly turns heated. She pulls back, breathing deeply, and her cheeks are flushed.

"Hey there," she breathlessly says.

"Hey," I say back, grinning at her.

"Are you going to invite me in?"

"Shit, yeah sorry, please." I step to the side and flick my hand inside indicating her to enter.

She walks past me and I'm assaulted with the smell of Chinese and Marlee's perfume. I need to find what it is and stock up on it, as it's my most favorite smell in the world. My eyes drop to her sexy as sin denim-covered ass as she sashays into my apartment. My tongue darts out, suddenly I'm hungry…and not for Chinese.

Closing the door, I follow behind her into my apartment. I can't resist and I give her ass a squeeze. She squeals in shock and when she looks over her shoulder at me, she smiles. It lights up her face and sets my insides on fire. My conversation with Kasey and Kody comes crashing back to me, and I unequivocally realize I am head over heels in love with Marlee Adams.

She places the food and beer on the island countertop and turns to face me. She lifts her hand and with her finger beckons me to her. Without hesitating, I place one foot in front of the other and walk over to her, she drapes her arms around my shoulders and gazes into my eyes. "I missed you."

A smile breaks free. "You saw me yesterday," I remind, as I wrap my arms around her waist, pulling her closer to me.

"That was forever ago," she pouts.

We silently gaze at one another. As I stare into her baby blues, I see deep into her soul, and I get the feeling that she feels exactly like I do. Lowering my head, I gently place my lips on hers for a slow, sensual kiss. When I pull back, I think, *Fuck it.* I open my mouth to say those three words that I haven't spoken since Ma, when there's another knock at the door.

"Fuck," I mumble but Marlee, excitedly says, "It's here!"

Squinting, I look inquisitively at her. She taps the tip of my nose and steps away to answer my front door. She has her hand on the handle when she turns and says to me, "Cover your eyes, I have a surprise for you."

"What?" I ask like a dummy.

"Close your eyes." We stare intently at one another. "Please," she adds.

With a sigh and a grin, I huff, "Fine." And I close my eyes.

"Cover them too," she requests.

My eyes pop open. "Really?"

She nods. "Really, really." There's another knock at the door. "Now, Grainger," she sternly warns.

Once again, I huff, "Fine." Lifting my hands, I close my eyes and cover them.

"Thank you," she cheerily says as she opens the door. I hear them quietly murmuring, followed by shuffling. A few minutes later the door closes.

"Can I open them yet?" I whine. I'm not fond of surprises and the feeling of the unknown is unnerving.

"Not just yet, give me a sec." I listen closely to try and figure out what's she's doing, but she's as quiet as a mouse right now. I hear her plug something in and then a switch flicks and she quietly says, "Perfect."

I feel her approaching me and I go to lower my arm, but she reaches forward and slams her hands against mine. "Not yet."

With her hand still on mine, over my eyes, she guides me into the living room. We come to a stop; she links her fingers with mine, and removes her hand from my eyes. "Surprise," she whispers.

Blinking a few times, I can't believe what's before me. Adorned in bright white Christmas lights is a four-foot Fraser fir Christmas tree, and beside it, a box of ornaments and on the top is an angel; it looks just like the one from my childhood. "Marlee," I mumble, I don't know what else to say. This is the first time in nineteen years I've had a tree, that I've actually cared about Christmas. That I feel the Christmas spirit."

Turning to Marlee, she gazes lovingly at me. Happiness etches her face and I'm pretty sure the grin she's sporting is a mirror image of mine. "Thank you," I whisper.

"You are welcome. I wanted to do something to surprise you after the amazing weekend we just had together. It's not much but…"

"No, Marlee," I say, as I cup her face in my palms. "It's everything. It's perfect." Lowering my lips to hers, I kiss her deeply. She places her arms around my waist and presses herself into me. Lowering my palms from her face, I place my hands under her ass and tap. She jumps up and wraps her legs around my waist and drapes her arms around my neck. Our lips crash together. Our teeth bumping as I walk backward to the couch and sit down with her straddling me.

Running my hands up her back, I slide under her shirt and when my palm makes contact with her skin, I feel a spark. Marlee must feel it too because she moans into my mouth and begins to grind herself on my dick, which is now rock-hard.

She slides her hands under the waistband of my pants and grips my cock. This time I moan into her mouth. I snake my hands between us and flip open the button on her jeans, lower her fly, and slide my hand inside her pants. I cup her mound, her underwear is soaked with arousal. I slide my hand and up and down her panties and feel the material moisten under my touch.

"Please, Gage," she begs, as she grinds herself on my hand. She hops off of me and quickly strips off her jeans, underwear, sweater, and bra. She's standing before me in nothing but her Santa hat.

"Fuck me, you are gorgeous, Marlee."

She grins at me as she lowers to her knees and pulls down my lounge pants. My cock springs free. She licks her lips and lowers her head toward my cock. Her tongue darts out and she licks the head. I groan when she sucks the tip between her lips, slowly sliding my cock into her warm, wet mouth. My hands grip her head and I guide her up and down. Her eyes are locked on mine as she continues to suck me.

"Fuuuuck," I moan, throwing my head back. Reaching forward, I lift her up so she's standing before me. "I want to come inside you," I moan. She steps toward me, straddles my legs, and lowers herself onto my cock. We watch as her pussy envelops my dick, when she's fully seated on me, her eyes flick up to mine. We stare at one another as she begins to ride me. Resting her hands on my shoulders for support, she slides up and down my dick. Her pussy hugging me tighter and tighter with each motion. Her body tenses and she screams, "Gaaaaaage," as her orgasm rips through her body. Seeing the pure look of ecstasy on her face pushes me over the edge and I come. Pistoning my hips into her as I ride out my release.

She rests her forehead on mine. "Merry Christmas, Gage," she breathless shares.

"It's not Christmas yet," I murmur back in reply.

"Everyday with you is like Christmas, Gage. I can't remember the last time I was this happy." She pauses and leans back. "I...I love you, Gage Grainger"

My mouth drops open in shock...she feels the same way.

She swallows deeply. "I don't expect you to say any—" I don't let her finish. I slam my lips against hers, grip her cheeks tightly, and I kiss her with everything I have. When I pull back, I gaze into her eyes, which are shimmering and reflecting the Christmas tree lights.

"I love you too." I reply, her eyes bug open at my declaration. "I realized this morning that I am head over heels in love with you." She smiles brightly back at me and I know that this is real. This is real fucking love and I could not be happier. "I planned to tell you tonight, I didn't plan on telling you while we were naked and my dick was inside of you, but in all honesty, it couldn't have been a more prefect moment. Marlee, you make me a better person, and for that I will eternally be grateful. I love you with my whole heart and soul, Marlee Adams."

"Ohh, Gage," she sighs, cupping my cheek. "I love you with my whole heart and soul too."

We spend the rest of the night naked on the couch, eating cold Chinese, drinking beer, and watching the snow fall outside. The night could not be more prefect.

When I wake the next morning, I'm alone on the couch. I look to the coffee table and see a note from Marlee.

THANK YOU FOR THE MOST WONDERFUL NIGHT.
HAD AN EARLY MEETING I HAD TO GET TO, I'LL CALL YOU LATER TODAY.
LOVE YOU.
M XOXOX

With a smile on my face, I walk into my bedroom and turn the shower on. While I wait for the water to heat, I stare at my reflection in the mirror. I'm smiling, but for once, it's reflected back in my eyes too. I am absolutely happy and nothing can take that away from me…or so I thought.

CHAPTER 13

Later that day, I'm at my desk when my office phone rings, it's coming from reception. "This is Gage," I answer when I pick up, holding the phone between my ear and neck so I can finish this e-mail.

"Gage, it's Stacey at reception. There's a Sullivan Grainger here to see you."

Taking a deep breath, I close my eyes and exhale deeply. "I'll be right there, Stacey."

Slamming the phone down, I rest my elbow on the edge of my desk and pinch the bridge of my nose, mumbling, "Fuck." Pushing my chair back, I stand up and head out of my office toward my dad…the last person in the world I want to see.

Walking into reception, I stop midstep when I see Dad talking and laughing with Marlee. My blood boils at seeing this. Marlee looks up and smiles at me, for a brief moment her smile calms me, and then my eyes flick to Dad and my blood simmers once again.

"Dad," I tersely say between clenched teeth. Marlee's eyes flick to mine and her mouth drops open. She's either shocked at the anger in my voice, to the fact I just referred to this man as my father, or both.

"Gage," Dad replies.

With my eyes locked on Marlee's I say. "Dad, I'll be with you in a moment." Without waiting for a reply, I add, "Marlee, a word?" My voice comes out angrier than I intended.

Her face is etched with worry and confusion. She looks to Dad and smiles at him. *He doesn't deserve your smiles*, I think to myself, as Marlee and I walk around the corner. "What are you doing here?" I briskly ask.

"I just finished up a meeting with Chelle and Kasey, I was about to ask Stacey if you were free when I heard someone ask for you. I was shocked when I realized that that someone was your dad. You told me you had no family."

"I don't," I snap in reply.

"Then that man out there isn't your father?"

"He might be my sperm donor, but he's not my father. I lost my family when I was ten. The day my Ma died."

"I don't understand, Gage."

"You wouldn't," I snap again, "You had the perfect life. Perfect parents. Perfect everything. Me? I had a drunk for father, who didn't give two shits about me. With that accident, my whole world imploded. The day she died, I lost what little father I had."

"Gage," she says, her voice laced with pity. She reaches for me and I pull back.

"No, I don't want your pity."

"Gage, no, that's—"

"Save it, Marlee. I've heard it all over the last twenty years. I don't need to hear it from you too."

"Gage," she snaps back at me. "You do not get to speak to me that way. When you've pulled your head out of your ass. You know where to find me." She turns and storms away from me.

Taking a deep breath, I mumble, "Fuck." Turning on my heel, I chase after her and shout, "Marlee, wait!"

By the time I make it back to reception, the elevator doors are closing and the look of hurt on her face as a tear cascades down her cheek crushes me. Closing my eyes, I breathe in deeply and run my fingers across my forehead, releasing the tension building; that is until my father speaks. "Gage?"

My head snaps toward the man before me, and I look over at him. I really look at him. He doesn't look anything like what I last remember, it must be at least six years since I have seen him. "Dad, what are you doing here?"

"I...I..." he stutters. "I need to speak to you, Son."

"Stop calling me that," I snarl. "You lost your son twenty years ago," I spit back at him, my rage once again simmering toward the man in front of me.

"Please, Gage. Can we just go somewhere private and talk?" I look around and see Stacey staring at me, she sadly smiles before picking up the phone.

Looking over at Dad, I stare at him, and for the first

time in twenty years, I feel sad for the man standing before me. "Fine, you have ten minutes."

Turning my back on him, I storm back toward my office. Walking in, I sit at my desk and wait for Dad. Resting my elbows on the edge of my desk, I lower my head into my hands. The click of the door closing causes me to look up. Dad takes a seat across from me. He's breathing heavily and is quite pale. "Can I get you some water?" I reluctantly ask him.

"No, I'm fine. I won't take up much of your time."

The room falls silent. The air is thick with animosity and it's quite awkward.

"Son—"

"Stop fucking calling me that. You have no right to call me Son."

"Gage, please." He pauses, staring at me, and I shake/nod my head in a 'hurry the fuck up and speak' way. "As I said the other day, I have cancer and I'm dying. I...I'm sorry."

"And as I said the other day, you don't get to make deathbed amends. It's too late. You've had twenty years to be a father to me, and instead you drank your life away. You left me to fend for myself. You left me to grieve for Ma by myself; I was ten fucking years old! I was trapped in the damn car with her. To this day, I have that vacant stare she had on her face etched clearly in my mind, like it was just yesterday." I pause and take a breath. "I lost you even more that day. I know you hated that I was born and when she died, it only cemented your hatred for me."

"Gage, no."

"Dad, you've had your ten minutes. I'd like you to leave."

We stare at one another, he sadly smiles at me and stands to leave. "I hope you can work things out with that young lass. I can see you care for her deeply, the look in your eyes when you spoke to her reminded me of when I first met your mother, before…" He doesn't finish what he was going to say; he just nods at me, sadly smiles, turns, and slowly walks out.

Sitting in my chair, I stare at the door and think about everything that just transpired. I was such a dick to Marlee; all she was trying to do was offer me comfort and I threw it back in her face like an asshole. And then there's Dad, he was nice, almost fatherly. That's confusing enough, he was rarely fatherly before Ma died, after her death he became an even bigger asshole, and I was an inconvenience.

"Fuuuuck!" I growl to my empty office as I run my fingers through my hair, gently pulling to cause myself pain and possibly ease the tension…but it doesn't work. I'm still agitated over Dad and pissed off with how I spoke to Marlee.

The day drags by ever so slowly and just before five, I pack up and leave.

Stopping in at Bin 501, I quickly speak to Kody about a wine that will accompany my apology to Marlee. He hands me a blah blah Verdelho and assures me that Marlee will love it. He tells me to grab some salami, cheese, and bread and I'll have a gourmet meal to go with my apology. As for the apology itself, he told me I'm on my own there; asshole.

With the wine and hamper in hand, I walk across the road. Someone is coming out so I can slip in and surprise Marlee. In the elevator on the way up to her floor, my heart begins to race erratically and I'm nervous as hell. I really don't want to lose her. I just hope my outburst from earlier hasn't ruined what we have started. I really love this woman, and I'm going to fight tooth and nail to prove my love to her.

CHAPTER 14

RAISING MY HAND, I KNOCK ON HER DOOR, GRATEFUL KASEY gave me her apartment number when I called and groveled on the drive here. A few moments later the door opens, when I see Marlee I feel like an even bigger asshole. Her eyes are red and puffy from crying, there are mascara tracks down her cheeks, and she looks broken…all because of me.

"Marlee, babe, I'm so sorry I was such a dick to you. That man brings the worst out in me."

"You can't blame your father for everything, Gage."

I stare at Marlee, shocked at what she said, but a part of me knows she's right. "I know, you're right." I pause. "Can I come in and tell you the truth about my father?"

She looks at me but doesn't say anything. "If it sweetens the offer, I also have this." Raising the wine and hamper for her to see.

"Depends."

"On what?" I hesitantly ask. I'm currently worried she's going to turn me away.

"What type of wine you have?"

"It's a vermelho. Kody assures me it's divine."

"Never heard of vermelho." She grins at me. "But if you mean Verdelho and Kody recommended it, then I'll allow you to enter."

"Thank you." I step into her apartment, stop in front of her, and place a kiss on her cheek. "I really am sorry."

"I know," she sadly says, her voice showing how much I've hurt her.

She steps away from me and walks into her kitchen. My eyes follow her and as usual, drift down to her ass. She's still in her work clothes, and today she's rocking a sexy as fuck, dark blue pencil skirt that hugs her curves perfectly and a white blouse with ruffles.

I step in the kitchen, place everything on the counter, and turn to her. "You look lovely today, Marlee."

She smiles at me. "Thank you."

Stepping toward her, I wrap my arms around her waist and she places her arms over my shoulders. "I really am sorry for how I spoke earlier today. It was a shock to see you laughing with him. I can't remember the last time I did that with him."

"Why do you hate him so much?"

"Where do I begin?"

"At the beginning, generally," she teases, sticking her

tongue at me cheekily, seeing her do that, I know we will be okay.

"Let's get this set up and then I'll tell you."

"Deal." She grabs two stemless wine glasses, while I take the hamper into the living room and place it on the coffee table. Sitting on the rug, I pull out the food and arrange the packages on the table. Marlee joins me with the wine in a bucket and our glasses. Taking the bottle from her, I uncork it, pour us each a glass, and hand one to her. She takes the glass from me and our fingers touch, a spark jolts through me, setting my body ablaze. With our eyes locked on one another, we silently drink our wine.

"You picked well, Mr. Grainger."

"Thank you, Ms. Adams. But as we both know, I know crap all when it comes to wine," I remind with a wink in reply. "But I'm growing to know and appreciate wines… especially vermelho"

Still staring at one another, she nods and smirks at me. Closing my eyes, I take a deep breath, when I open them, I stare out the window and spill everything. "My father is an alcoholic. He'd have the occasional beer before Ma passed. When he lost his job, he started to heavily drink. After Ma died, it got worse. When I lost her, I lost him too. Not that I really had him before hand. He'd put me down at every opportunity. To me, he'd treat Ma like crap but she loved him unconditionally." I shake my head. "I never understood why Ma was with him. I think I can count on one hand the number of happy memories that involve the three of us." She reaches over and squeezes my hand. "It's funny, to this day, I don't think he and I have spoken about her since she passed."

"Gage, he's probably grieving himself. Yes, he shut you

out, and that sucks ass, but they obviously loved each other deeply, and when she died, a part of him died too. He probably didn't know how to cope without her." I go to say something, but she raises her hand to stop me. "I'm not excusing his behavior, but losing the one you love must be tough."

"I guess so."

"And just think, you wouldn't be the wonderful, caring man you are if all of that had not happened."

Marlee leans forward, grabs the wine from the bucket and tops off our glasses. She sits back next to me and raises her glass. "A toast, to Mrs. Grainger. The best mom a little boy could ask for."

With a sad smile, I clink my glass against hers and whisper, "To Ma."

We sit in comfortable silence for a while; drinking our wine and watching the snowfall. She snuggles into my side and we talk about the toy drive tomorrow. I'm actually excited to be involved this year, and I know that Ma would be impressed, I laugh.

"What are you laughing at?" she enquires.

"Ma would be so happy to know I'm actually helping. She always went above and beyond when it came to Christmas and the less fortunate. She'd bake hundreds of cookies for the church, and then she'd drop gifts off to the shelters around the area." I smile. "You and she would have gotten along like a house on fire. She'd love you, I just like I do."

She looks over at me and smiles. "I love you too." She leans up and places her lips against my cheek. "She'd be so proud of you, Gage." She sits back down, and we continue to watch the snow fall, drink our wine, and nibble on the platter.

When the wine is finished and the hamper is empty, we rearrange the pillows and grab the duvet off the bed. We get comfortable on the floor and snuggle together. The animosity and angst from when I first arrived has disappeared. Both Marlee and I are now relaxed and back in our happy bubble. I like our bubble and I hope it never pops.

We finish another bottle of wine, and by the window we make love all night long.

CHAPTER 15

It's toy drive day and I'm amazed at what we, well, Chelle, Kasey, and Marlee, have pulled off in such a short amount of time. Everything is going to plan, until Marlee receives a call that threatens to derail everything.

"No, no, no," Marlee wails as she throws her phone down on the table.

"What's wrong?" The three of us ask in unison.

"We have no Santa!" Marlee cries.

"Huh?" I ask.

Kasey says, "Shit."

And Chelle just shrugs nonchalantly and shoves another strip of licorice in her mouth.

"We have no Santa. The one we had booked just got hit by a car on his way to pick up the suit."

"Ohh, crap balls," Kasey says. "What are we going to do now?"

"Do you need a Santa? Can't we just chuck the presents under the tree, let the kids have at them, and be done with it?" I ask.

"No," Marlee snaps. "After the kids do their Christmas parade, Santa was to arrive and give out the presents. The kids have been so excited to meet Santa."

"I've got it," Kasey says, looking at me, and I don't like the look she has on her face. "You," she points at me, "will dress as Santa for us."

"Yes!" Marlee excitedly shouts.

Chelle laughs, "I'll pay to see that."

"Nope, nah ah, not happening."

"Yes, it's happening," Kasey affirms.

"Nah, uh, Buttercup." She glares at me, digs her phone out of her pocket, and dials. "Babe, it's me, can you stop at the costume store on Stanton Blvd and pick up the Santa outfit?" She stops and listens for a moment. "No, Gage is suiting up." Through the phone I can hear Kody laughing his ass off. "Thanks, babe. See you soon."

"All sorted," Kasey gloats.

"You owe me," I warn Kasey. She shrugs her shoulders and goes back to wrapping presents.

Marlee walks over and wraps her arms around me. "Thank you so much, Gage. This would have been a disaster if you hadn't agreed to do this."

"I didn't actually agree. You three railroaded me."

Marlee leans into my ear and huskily whispers, "I'll

make it worth your while tonight," before nipping my earlobe. My dick immediately sparks to life.

"You better," I huff.

Three hours later, I'm dressed as Santa and handing out the gifts. This afternoon has been so much fun, not that I'll tell the girls that. Seeing the enjoyment on the kids' faces makes it all worthwhile, but seeing the joy on Marlee's face, that's the icing on the cake.

After handing the last gift out, I say my goodbyes to all the kids. They excitedly wave and scream when I exit the room; it is deafening but thrilling to see the excitement on their little faces.

I'm in the back office, about to change, when the door swings open. Spinning around, I see Marlee standing there. She has the biggest smile on her face; she stalks toward me, pulls the fake beard down, grips my cheeks, and kisses me. She covers my mouth with her lips, sweeping her tongue inside, tangling with mine. This kiss is hot. She breaks the kiss and stares at me. "Thank you, Gage. You were the best Santa. Without you, this afternoon just wouldn't have been the same."

"I actually had fun, but don't tell Kasey that."

"Your secret is safe with me, Santa. Can I just say, you are the sexiest Santa I have ever seen."

"Well, you are the sexiest elf I have ever kissed."

"How many elves have you kissed?"

"A Santa never tells," I cheekily reply.

We stare at one another intently; the air around us thick with lust, arousal, and desire. The moment is broken when

Kasey walks in. "Dude, you rocked it. Who knew you would be an amazing Santa?"

"I did," Marlee says, staring hungrily a me. Her eyes roaming over my body. If Kasey wasn't here, I'd lift up Marlee's dress and fuck the life out of her.

"Well, yeah, whatever, get changed; since it's Friday, we are all heading to Bin 501 for celebration drinks." Before we can reply, she grabs her bag and walks out, slamming the door behind her.

Thirty minutes later, Marlee and I walk into Bin 501, hand in hand. We find everyone in the back and head over. When they notice me, in unison everyone chants, "HO! HO! HO!"

"Shut up, assholes," I scoff, as I pull the finger at everyone, but secretly I'm enjoying the attention. This is the first Christmas in twenty years that I'm happy, and it's all to do with the woman next to me. Draping my arm over her shoulder, I pull her into me and place a kiss on the side of her head.

Kody and Branson walk over to the table with bottles of red and white wine. They place them down and begin to open them. Branson looks to Marlee and me. "Red or white?"

"White," we both answer.

Marlee leans into me and whispers, "And what's it called again?"

"Vermelho," I reply with a smirk.

"That's my new fav wine," she says back, placing a kiss on my jawline before she turns her attention to Branson, and they start talking about wine and shit.

With a glass in hand, I walk to the side of the group and watch. I'm not really a people person; I prefer to blend into the background. Kasey spies me, grabs a bottle of white, and walks over to me. Without asking, she tops off my glass and stares at me. "What?" I ask.

"You look happy."

My eyes drift over to Marlee. "I am. I don't think I have ever been this happy."

She rests her palm on my arm, "I'm happy for you, Gage. You deserve to be," she nods her head toward Marlee, "and so does she."

"She's it for me, Kasey. I know I've only known her for a few weeks but, I can't explain it, I just know."

"Dude, I totally know what you mean. If you guys have what Kody and I have, then I'm happy for you both."

"Thanks, Kase," I say, as I pull her in for a sideways hug. My eyes are locked on Marlee and I watch her walk over to us.

"Get your hands off my man," she playfully teases.

"Babe, he's all yours. Especially, when I have that hunk-o-spunk over there." We look over to see Kody, Branson, and Chelle laughing. Kody looks over to us and you can see the love in his eyes for his fiancée...it's similar to the love I have for Marlee.

She wraps her arm around my waist, she feels amazing in my arms. As I stare at her, a fucking crazy idea forms; I totally blame it on the wine I've just drunk. I lean in and whisper, "Wanna get out of here? I have a surprise for you."

She looks up at me and nods. Grabbing Marlee's hand, we say goodbye to everyone, and I drag her out of the bar. "I think you are going to like what I have in store for you," I whisper into her ear as we wait for our cab.

She squeezes my ass and coos, "As long as it involves your cock, then I'm sure I will."

Grinning at her, I don't say anything in reply, I just raise my eyebrows suggestively at her and she giggles. Her giggle shoots straight to my cock, and suddenly, I can't wait to get back to her place.

After what feels like an eternity, a cab finally pulls up. We climb in and I give the driver Marlee's address. We turn to one another and make out like teenagers. We totally could have walked, but I'm horny and excited for what I have in store.

♡

CHAPTER 16

STANDING IN MARLEE'S BEDROOM, WITH MY BACK TO THE door, I'm stark naked, except for a Santa hat and a red present sack which I have slung over my right shoulder. My heart is erratically racing—not with nerves—but excitement. Shaking my head, I take a deep breath. "Now or never," I mumble to myself, but before I can sing out that I have my surprise ready, Marlee yells though the door, "Can I come in yet?"

The sounds of her voice zings through my body. Taking a deep breath, I close my eyes, and whisper to myself, "Let's do this."

Confidently, I shout, "Yep, you can come in now."

The room is silent, except for my nervous, heavy

breathing. The door clicks open and I can hear Marlee's footsteps approaching, but she doesn't say anything. I feel her presence even though I can't see her; I can always sense she's near. She hasn't spoken a word and I'm too nervous to speak.

She's right behind me. The air around us is electric. She squeezes my ass, causing me to yelp in surprise. I feel her breath at my ear. "Ho. Ho. Ho," she huskily purrs, her hot breath causing my cock to twitch in excitement. She snakes her hand around my stomach and circles my navel. I drop the sack and reach back, threading my fingers in her hair. She kisses my neck and traces a line down my stomach toward my cock. She grips me tight in her fist and strokes. I can feel her smiling behind me. I try to spin around to see her, but she whispers, "Uhhh uh, let me do this." She nibbles on my neck, as I close my eyes and lose myself in the moment.

With my eyes still closed, I concentrate on her touch. Her stokes are light but frenzied. I don't want to come like this. Gripping her hand, I pause her motion and spin around. My mouth drops open at the vision before me. She is wearing a red and white mesh teddy, Santa hat, and what I'm hoping is a G-string. My eyes drift down her body and her feet are encased in the sexiest pair of black fuck-me heels I have ever seen.

"Fuck me," I mumble.

She leans forward and presses her lips against mine. "Let me unwrap your present first, and then I can," she whispers, her voice deep and ever so sexy.

Stepping back, she slides her finger under the strap of her teddy and traces along the edge. My eyes lock on her finger as she skims the tip, ever so lightly, across the top of her breasts. Circling her nipple through the mesh before flipping open the clasp between her tits. The material falls away and her breasts spring free. Licking my lips, I want nothing more than to step forward and bury my face between them. I've always been a tits and ass man, and Marlee has the most amazing tits and ass ever. She slides the material down her arms and the teddy flutters to the carpet, pooling at her feet. She sensually slides her hands down her sides, into the band of her panties, hooking her finger on the edge, she pulls them down her legs and steps out of them. She is now standing before me in nothing but a Santa hat and heels…sexiest thing I have ever seen.

"That's not fair," I whine, "you unwrapped my present."

She shrugs her shoulders at me before stepping forward. Her nipples are erect and she's close enough to me that I can feel the heat of them on my skin. Wrapping my arms around her, I tug her into my chest and slam my lips against hers. She drapes her arms over my shoulders, pressing our bodies closer together. She deepens the kiss and moans into my mouth as our tongues slide and explore each other's mouth.

Stepping back, I sit on the edge of the bed and pull Marlee so she's straddling me. She shimmies forward, her pussy precariously close to my erection. She begins to move her hips, seeking out my cock. Grinning into the kiss, I flip her onto her back, spread her legs wide with my knees, and thrust inside of her. We both moan at the intrusion as I begin the piston in and out of her. She wraps her legs around me, allowing me in deeper. She wriggles her hips beneath me, matching my movements.

"I'm coming," she moans. "Gaaaaaage," she squeals, as

her climax detonates. When she groans my name and squeezes my ass, it sets me off and I come inside her.

"Wow," I murmur into her neck, as I come back to Earth.

"Wow, indeed," she breathlessly replies. "You really do rock as Santa."

We both laugh, as I flop back onto the bed and shimmy us up to the headboard and pillows. She rolls off me, onto her side, and snuggles into me.

"I love you, Marlee," I whisper, as I place a kiss on the side of her head.

"Love you too," she mumbles before falling asleep in my arms…this is now my most favorite way to fall asleep: Marlee naked and snuggled into my side.

We spend the weekend naked and fucking like rabbits. We christen every surface in her and my apartments. We've never been closer than we are now, and each night we drift off to sleep blissfully happy in each others' arms…but our bliss bubble pops the very next day.

CHAPTER 17

It's Monday and Christmas is just over a week away. The morning is slowly dragging by. I'm staring out the window when my phone pings with a text, I smile when I see it's Marlee.

Marlee: *Wanna do lunch?*

Gage: *I wanna do you...*

Marlee: *So that's a yes?*

Gage: *Can't do lunch.*

Marlee: *Dinner then?*

Gage: *Dinner is always a yes with you, baby. When and where?*

Marlee: *Ummm, my place. Anytime after work*

Gage: *It's a date.*
Marlee: *smiley face emoji*
Gage: *thumbs-up emoji*

With a smile on my face, I know I won't get a reply. Marlee thinks the thumbs-up emoji is rude, but to my surprise my phone pings again.

Marlee: *middle finger emoji*

I can't help but laugh, this woman is perfect for me. With renewed vigor, I jump in and finalize the marketing for February and Valentine's Day. Before I know it, it's home time. *Finally.*

Racing home, I jump in the shower, quickly wash and change before I head over to Marlee's for dinner, and dessert will be her.

Having her across the road is great because I can get there quickly as possible.

As usual, someone is coming out so I can sneak in and surprise her. With a pep in my step, which happens quite often lately, I exit the elevator and walk down the hallway to her door. I can hear voices inside and deflate a little as I wanted it to be just us this evening. Raising my hand, I knock on the door. It swings open and my mouth drops open when I see who belongs to the other voice.

"Hello, Gage," he says.

My eyes are locked on his. My blood is boiling, as I snap my gaze to Marlee. She has a worried look on her face, and so she should. "Why is he here, Marlee?"

I'm seething. This is not how I expected my night to go.

"Gage, please." She carefully places her hand on my arm, "Come in and I'll explain."

"Nope, I'm good here."

"Don't be an ass," she snaps, "Get in my apartment now."

"I like her," he declares to me.

"No," I snarl, as I push past Marlee toward the one person who I never thought I would see in Marlee's apartment. "You don't get to side with her. It's bad enough that you are here." Pausing, I take a deep calming—not so calming—breath. "Why are you here, Dad?"

"Marlee invited me."

"What?" I snap, my blood beginning to boil with anger.

Marlee walks over to me, grabs my hand, and laces our fingers together. "Gage, please. Sit down and I'll explain."

Pulling my hand from hers, I throw my hands in the air in an exasperated manner. "Yes, please explain how the one person in the world—who I have no fucking desire to see—is in your apartment." Walking over to the window, I then spin around in anger. "And how the fuck are you two in contact?"

"Watch your tone, Gage," Dad warns. "Marlee called me earlier," Dad explains.

My head snaps to hers. "How in the hell did you get his number?"

A guilty look washes over her face. "I got his number out of your phone."

"You what?" I snap.

"Gage, don't speak to her like that. Your Ma raised you better than that."

My eyes snap to his, and I seethe, shaking my head,

"You don't get to speak to me about Ma. You lost that right the day she died. The day she died is the day I lost you too. I know you wish it was me who died, and not her. You made that known every day you ignored me. Everyday that you chose to drink rather than be my father. I lost both parents that day, and I don't need you now."

"I know you don't owe me anything, Gage. And I see that you have grown into a great man, someone your mother would be proud of. I regret many things in my life, but my biggest regret was not being there when you needed me. Your mother would be ashamed of me."

"No shit," I scoff.

"I'd love nothing more than your forgiveness but..." He doesn't finish his sentence because there's nothing else to say. Looking over to him, I stare at the man before me. In his eyes, I see regret and grief.

"Dad, it's too late. I...I just can't."

Walking to the door, I open it and walk out. Leaving Marlee and Dad alone. Before the door closes, I hear Dad cry. It does pull at my heartstrings to hear him like that, but at this very moment, everything he put me through is vividly playing in my mind. Pressing the button for the elevator, I wait.

A door opens behind me and I turn to see who it is, Marlee stand's in the doorway. "Gage—"

"No." I raise my hand to stop her. "Just no, I...I need to be alone right now. I don't want to say something in the heat of the moment that I'll regret. But I will say this, this is a giant betrayal right now." Her face pales, her eyes well with tears, and she gasps at my words.

The elevator dings and the doors open, without saying

anything else, I climb in. As the doors close, Marlee blubbers, "I'm sorry, Gage, I thought I was helping."

The elevator doors shut and I let out the breath I was holding. I storm across the road and up to my apartment. As soon as I get inside, I grab a bottle of Jack, open it, and swig. It burns on the way down and it's exactly what I need.

Flopping onto my couch, I run my fingers through my hair and lean back into the cushions. My eyes land on the only photo I have of Ma and me. Hopping up, I grab the frame and sit back down. I stare at the photo and my eyes well with tears. "Why, Ma, why did you have to leave us?"

Grabbing the bottle by the neck, I drink again. Slamming the bottle on the coffee table, I rest my elbows on my knees and lower my head to my hands. When I lift it up, my gaze lands on the tree, specifically the angel on top and a conversation I had with Ma comes flooding back to me.

...December 5th, 1998

"Why does Dad hate us?" I ask Ma.

"Your father doesn't hate us, Gage. He's just misunderstood."

"He's so mean. Why do you stay?"

"Gage, when you are older and meet 'the one' this will make much more sense. When you love someone unconditionally, you look past their flaws and see into their soul. Your father has a kind soul under his rough exterior. He swept me off my feet when I was nineteen, and I thank my lucky stars everyday. Not just because he gave me you, but because of the little things that you don't see, or appreciate, because you are only a child. One day you will know what I mean. Yes, they will do things that

will make you want to smother them with a pillow, but at the same time, they would lay their life down for you."

"I don't see any of that in him," I whine.

"That's because, young man, you are ten and not in love with him. You see him as a father and a father only."

"But—"

"There are no buts when it comes to love, Gage. Even when they do things to hurt you, it comes from a place of love. If you could see your father though my eyes, you'd see him how I do. A gentle soul who has a unique way of showing his love. Underneath his hardness is a man who loves unconditionally."

With a smile on my face, I walk over to the window and stare across to Marlee's building. Looking down to the street, I see her and Dad on the sidewalk. A cab is waiting, they chat for a few moments and then he climbs in. She stands on the street and watches it pull away.

She looks up and I know she can't see me, but I can feel her stare on me. Digging into my pocket, I pull my phone out and quickly dial her number. My eyes are locked on hers, I watch as she pulls her phone out. She hesitates before she answers. "Hello," she meekly says.

"Marlee, babe—"

"I'm coming up, Gage Grainger, and you will let me in, and you *will* let me say what I want to say."

"Ooookay."

"Good, see you in a few."

Hanging up, I watch as she marches across the road and over to my building. *This should be interesting,* I think to myself as I walk over to the buzzer to let her in.

CHAPTER 18

As soon as I open the door, Marlee storms into my apartment. Closing the door, I follow her into the living room, where she spins on her heel. "Gage, I'm sorry I went behind your back, but you need closure. I thought if you and your dad could clear the air, then it would all be good. I didn't realize that you were an immature jackass who holds grudges."

"You done?" I snarkily ask.

"Are you done being an immature jackass douche-hole?" she spits back at me.

"Are you?"

"Clearly you are still immature, Gage."

"Says the immature one."

"Oh My God, really?"

"Really, really," I playfully reply, in the donkey from *Shrek* tone.

"You are so frustrating."

"Sexily frustrating," I reply with a wink. "But seriously, you are right. I do need to speak to him."

Her mouth drops open in shock. "Wow, I thought I would have had to fight harder on this. What's changed in the past thirty minutes?"

"I remembered a conversation with Ma, it was just before she died. She told me why she loved him, he's just misunderstood, and underneath his rough exterior is a gentle soul."

"I think I would have loved your ma."

"And she would have loved you too."

"And I think she's right. I've only spent a little time with him, and I don't see the bad person you do. Sure, he's handled things in a shitty way, but deep down, Gage, he loves you."

Staring at her, I think about what she just said. "Yeah, maybe you're right."

"There's one way to find out for sure." I stare blankly at her, "You need to call him. Sit down and chat man-to-man. Father to son."

"I'm scared, Marlee. What if he…"

"What if what?"

"What if I haven't made him proud?"

"Gage," she tenderly says, cupping my cheek to placate me. "He will be. I wouldn't have fallen in love with you if you weren't an amazing human being. He will be proud."

"But—"

She places her finger on my lips. "No buts, now make that call."

Taking a deep breath, I dig my phone out of my pocket. Unlocking the screen, I bring up my contacts and scroll down to his. My finger hovers over his name, closing my eyes, I take a deep breath and dial.

"Hello?"

"Dad…"

"Gage, I'm so happy you called. I'm sorry for everything. Please don't be angry at Marlee, she was just trying to help. She reminds me so much of your mother, those two would get along like a house on fire," he says all of this in one breath.

"Dad," I yell. "It's okay. I'm not mad at her. And yes," I stare at her a smile, "she is very much like Ma. I was, umm, ahh, wondering if we can meet up tomorrow?"

"I'd love nothing more."

"Do you want to come here for dinner tomorrow night?"

"I'd really like that. Gage, I really am sorry."

"I know, Dad. I'm sorry too. We are both at fault here. Ma would be disappointed in both of us and our behavior."

He laughs, "She sure would. I can only imagine the lecture I will get when I'm reunited with her again."

When he says that, I remember he's sick and dying. "How are you doing?"

"I'm dying, there's not much else to say."

"Dad—"

"No, Gage, it's fine. I've made my peace with it. The last thing I wanted to do before I go is make amends with you. I guess I'm getting my final wish after all."

We both go quiet. This is too heavy for me right now. "I have to go, Dad, but I'll see you tomorrow night."

"You can count on it." He pauses. "I love you, Gage."

His words shock me. "Bye, Dad."

Hanging up, I place my phone on the counter. Marlee walks over to me and wraps her arms around my waist. "You did a good thing, Gage."

"I hope so. It was hard speaking to him, but he does sound different. He sounds like the Dad from the few happy memories I have."

"And tomorrow, you will have new memories to add."

I think about what she said, and I wonder if our conversation just now was a fluke, and if I'll be adding happy or sad memories tomorrow.

It's an hour after Dad was meant to be here and he's MIA. Shaking my head, I pour myself a drink and walk over to the windows. Looking down to the street, hoping to see him outside—scared and waiting to come up—but the street is empty, except for the mountains of snow. Last night there was a huge snowstorm. My phone rings, I'm tempted not to answer as I don't want to hear his excuses. I'm really not surprised that he didn't turn up. It's typical Dad. When I look at my phone it's an unknown number, so I answer. "Hello, this is Gage."

"Mr. Grainger. This is Dr. Ashton from The University of Chicago Medicine ER. We have your father, Sullivan Grainger, here. He was—"

"Is he okay?" I interrupt, my heart beating erratically at the news.

"He collapsed earlier today and hit his head. He's currently stable but he's asking for you."

"I'll be right there."

The doctor explains to me where to go when I arrive. Racing to my car, I jump in and head to the hospital. When I'm stopped at a red light, I call Marlee.

"Hey, sexy," she purrs.

"Hey, babe. That was just the welcome I needed." My voice is rushed and my tone sombre.

"What's wrong?"

"It's Dad. He's in the hospital."

"Ohh, Gage, do you need me to come with you?"

"I'm already on my way. I'm at a light and I just needed to hear your voice."

"Is he going to be okay?"

"The doctor didn't say much over the phone. I'll call you when I have more information. I love you, Marlee."

"Love you too, Gage. Please keep me posted, no matter what time it is."

I nod my head, I then remember I'm on the phone. "Will do. Bye, babe." Disconnecting the call, the light changes and I put my foot on the accelerator and drive to the hospital.

Arriving at the hospital, I park my car and race through the corridors to the ward the doctor said Dad was being moved too. Stopping at the nurses' desk, I'm huffing and puffing.

"Can I help you?" the nurse asks.

"Yes, Sullivan Grainger, has been admitted."

"You must be Sully's son?"

My eyes pop open in surprise. "You know who I am?"

"Yes. He talks about you often." She purses her lips,

before adding, "He's been wanting to reach out for a while but was scared too. After the news earlier this month, I'm guessing he did."

"What news?" I ask.

Now it's her turn for her eyes to pop open. "I, umm, thought you knew."

"Knew what?" I ask, my heart beating rapidly in my chest again.

"He's dying," she sadly informs.

"Well, I know that. That's why he reached out to me. Make amends on his deathbed and all that shit." My reply is harsher than I intended, but who does this woman think she is? She doesn't know me or our story. "Can you tell me where he is, please?"

She eyes me, sighs, and says, "Room seven-oh-two, to your left."

"Thank you," I say, turning on my heel I make my way toward Dad's room. When I get to the door, I take a deep breath and stare at the wood. Lifting my hand, I push the handle down and open the door. I'm not prepared for what I see. It's only been twenty-four hours since I saw him, but the man lying in the bed before me is not the man I saw last night, or remember. This man is frail looking. He looks like he's already dead. He must sense my presence and opens his eyes. When he see's me, they light up a fraction. "Gage," he softly whispers.

"Dad," I murmur, as my eyes well with tears. Walking over to the bed, I pull the chair closer and sit down. "Are you okay?"

"Fit as a fiddle," he says, with a slight smile.

"What happened?" I ask.

"I was on my way to the bus to get to your place when

I collapsed and hit my head. I pleaded with them to call you, but they were focused on stopping my head from bleeding. I didn't want you to think I wasn't coming." He pauses. "I'm sorry, I missed dinner."

"We can do dinner at my place another time."

We both stare at each other, silent. We each know that there will be no other dinner, Dad will not be leaving this hospital. My eyes well with tears again, "Dad, I...I don't want to lose you."

"I don't want to lose you either, Gage, but my time is up." He swallows, "I'm sorry I was such a shitty father; before and after her death."

Reaching out, I hold his hand in mine, then I rest my head next to him on the bed, and for the first time in years, I cry. With his other hand, he rubs my head, just like Ma did when I was little. This moment will be one I will treasure and remember forever.

Leaving the hospital just after midnight, I make my way home, but instead of going to my place, I go over to Marlee's. Calling her on the way, she's waiting in the foyer for me when I walk over to her building. She opens the door when she sees me and when I step inside, she envelops me in a hug. For the second time tonight, I breakdown in tears. She doesn't say anything, she just consoles me and it's exactly what I need.

When I've composed myself, we head up to her apartment. She leads me into her bedroom and strips off my clothes until I'm in just my boxer briefs. We climb into bed and snuggle, I drift off to sleep wrapped in Marlee's arms. Content and safe.

CHAPTER 19

THE NEXT MORNING, I WAKE BEFORE MARLEE. ROLLING TO MY side, I watch her sleep, in a non-creepy way. She smiles and whispers, "Are you watching me sleep?"

"Maybe," I say. Lifting my hand, I brush a lock of hair off her forehead and lean toward her. Placing my lips on hers, I kiss her gently. Rolling her so she is now on top of me, I grip her cheeks, close my eyes and deepen the kiss. We kiss for a while then I feel her hand grip my cock.

My eyes open and I see her baby blues hungrily gazing down at me. "Make love to me, Gage," she whispers.

Reaching down, I grip the hem of her shirt and lift it over to head. We are now both in our underwear. Our lips find one another again and we hungrily kiss. My cock is rock-hard. She rolls off me and we both quickly remove our underwear. She climbs back on top of me and lowers herself down on my dick.

Her pussy is warm and hugs my cock tightly. She begins to ride me, running her hands into her hair, thrusting her chest forward. Reaching up I cup and massage her breasts. Pulling her forward, I wrap my mouth around her nipple and suck. Marlee moans and the sound is pure bliss to my ears. Licking across her chest, I take her other nipple into my mouth and gently nip and suck. "Fuuuuck," she moans.

Sitting up, she wraps her legs around my waist and her arms around my neck. I wrap mine around her lower back. We stare at one another as she continues to ride me. Both our bodies tense at the same time and we simultaneously come. Each of us grunting out our release.

We stare at one another for a few moments before she whispers, "I love you."

"Love you too." I whisper back, as I gently place my lips against hers.

Marlee climbs off me and walks naked toward the ensuite. Moving to the edge of the bed, I stare at the carpet and hear the shower turn on. Sensing her, I look up and see her leaning against the doorframe. She stretches out her hand to me. Standing up, I link my fingers with hers, while she pulls me into the shower. She pushes me under the water, the temperature is perfect. Closing my eyes, I tilt my head back, and let the water wash over me.

Marlee's hands are suddenly on me and when I open my eyes, I see that she is washing me. We stare at one another and she continues to wash me. Once I'm clean, I grab her bodywash and do the same to her. We are both silent, but with our gestures and gaze, we have a silent conversation, it's exactly what I need and perfect.

We step out of the shower, grab our towels, and dry off. Pulling on my clothes from yesterday, I head to the kitchen and put on the coffee while Marlee gets dressed. Looking up, I smile. She's dressed casually in a pair of black skinny jeans and a white off the shoulder sweater thingy. "You look beautiful," I compliment.

"Thanks. You look pretty good too." She steps in front of me and rests her hands on my chest. "How you doing?"

I shrug my shoulders. "I honestly don't know."

"Well, let's have a coffee and then head to your place. You can get a change of clothes and we can head to the hospital."

"I have to work, and so do you."

"No," she shakes her head, "we have to go to the hospital and be with your dad. I've spoken to Kasey and she'll tell management. I've also just cleared it with my boss."

I'm stunned and speechless, no one since Ma has ever looked after me like this before. My lips lift in a smile. "What did I ever do to deserve you? Marlee, without you by my side right now, I'd be a mess." I wrap my arms around her waist and pull her in for a hug.

"I'm happy to be here for you, Gage." She looks up at me and places a kiss on my chin. "Now, let's get to it."

We have a quick coffee and then head over to my place, where I change my clothes and then we head to the hospital. Marlee and I walk down the corridor hand in hand; having her by my side makes this all that much easier. We pass the nurses' station and I smile at the nurse from last night. She smiles back at me, but at the same time looks shocked I'm here again.

We walk into Dad's room and he's asleep. "I'll go get coffee." Marlee whispers to me. She leaves the room and I take a seat by the window. Looking outside, I stare at the bleak sky.

"It's going to snow today," Dad says. Turning to face him, I smile. "The sky has that look about it."

"Ma teach you that too?" I ask.

He nods and begins to cough. Hopping up, I grab the water cup off the bedside table and pass it to him. He smiles at me and takes a sip. He looks sicker than when I left last night. It hurts my heart seeing him like this. It's funny, for years I wished he was dead, and now that he's on death's door, I don't want him to go.

The door swings open, and Marlee walks in. "Hey, Mr. Grainger," she says. "How you feeling today?" She hands me a coffee and sits on the chair next to me.

"Much better, now that you're here." Dad looks to me and smiles. "Don't let this one go, Gage. She's a keeper."

With a smile, I look at her and rest my palm on her leg and gently run my thumb back and forth. "I'm not planning on letting her go."

"Good, good," Dad says, he closes his eyes again and drifts off to sleep.

Marlee and I silently sit by his bed. The door opens an hour later and in walks Dad's doctor. "I'm Dr. Ashton, you must be Gage, Sully's son."

"Pleasure to meet you," I greet, standing up; I shake his hand. "This is my girlfriend, Marlee." I've never ever said that before and it feels really good to say it out loud and call her my girlfriend.

"Nice to meet you," he says, shaking her hand. "Can we talk in private?" he asks, looking at Marlee.

"I'll go get us more coffee," Marlee says. She places a kiss on my cheek and leaves me alone with the doctor and Dad, who now is awake.

"How you doing, Sully?" Dr. Ashton asks Dad.

"Dying, you?" Dad jokes.

"Dad," I scold.

"What? It's true." He pauses and sadly looks to me. "Gage, Son, I know I'm not leaving this hospital. My time is almost up."

"No, Dad, don't say that," I snap. Turning to the doctor I ask, "What more can we do?"

"Gage, I'm afraid your father is right. His time is nearly up. All we can do now is make him comfortable and wait."

"But—"

"Gage, don't fight it. I've accepted it, and now that you and I have mended things, I can die a happy man. I'm ready to be reunited with your mother."

"I'll leave you to it. Take it easy, Sully, and please let the nurses know it you need any more pain relief. We will do what we can."

Dad nods his head, but I can tell by the look in his eyes, he's going to tough it out. *Stubborn bastard*, I think to myself as I stare out the window. Taking a deep breath, I turn around and stare at him. "You know what tomorrow is?" He looks at me confused. "It's the twentieth," I mumble.

He nods his head at me and sadly smiles. "I think it's fate that tomorrow is the anniversary of when we lost her. It will also be the date I'm reunited with her." He pauses and swallows deeply, "It will also mean, you will have one day a year to grieve rather than two."

"Dad," I whine, just like I did when I was little.

"Gage, I may be dying but I can still yell at you."

"I'd like to see you try." I cheekily reply.

We stare at one another and then we both laugh, it feels good to laugh with him.

"Gage. Son, I just want to let you know that I'm glad to have reconnected with you. I wish it was under better circumstances, but I want to let you know that I'm proud of the man you've become, despite how I treated you. Your mother would be proud too. And that girl out there, don't let her go. When I look at the two of you, I see your mother and me when we first met. Don't become like me. Don't become jaded when life gives you lemons. Grab those lemons and make lemonade."

I laugh, "I thought you'd tell me to grab the tequila and salt."

"That's works too," he says, and again we both laugh.

Marlee and I spend the rest of the day with Dad. He sleeps a lot but when he is awake, he tells stories to Marlee and me of when Ma was alive.

We laugh.

We cry.

We are father and son.

It's perfect.

I'm glad to have these final happy memories with him.

After dinner, Marlee heads home and I stay with Dad. The nurses bring in a bed, but I pull the chair next to Dad and we watch Ma's favorite Christmas movie, *Miracle on 34th Street*, the original.

The movie has just finished, the credits are rolling and I look over at Dad. He smiles back at me and closes his eyes. A weird feeling washes over me and as I watch him, I know it's time.

Dad takes his last breath at 12:01 a.m. on December 20th, 2018.

CHAPTER 20

My dad is gone. I always thought when it happened, I'd be over the moon happy, but I'm not. I'm devastated beyond belief. Both my parents are gone, I'm all alone now. Thankfully, I have Marlee by my side. After it happened I called her, I was sitting in his room, staring out the window when she opened the door.

Looking up, I whisper, "He's really gone."

She walks over to me and envelops me in a hug. The floodgates open, and I cry. I cry like I did when Ma died. Marlee hugs me tighter and the comfort from her right now only makes me cry harder.

"I'm so sorry, Gage," she whispers into my neck. We pull apart and I see that she's crying too.

"Why are you crying?" I ask, as I wipe away her tears with the pad of my thumbs.

"Gage, you just lost your dad. It's the anniversary of your ma's death. It's a sad day."

"I'm all alone," I blubber.

"No, you're not, you have me." She places a kiss on my cheek and hugs me again.

The next three days are a blur. Marlee has been my rock, my everything. She organizes Dad's cremation and on the twenty-third, he's cremated. He didn't want a service and I'm thankful for that, I don't think I could handle a big affair.

After it's done, we head back to my place and spend the afternoon watching Christmas movies and drinking wine from the hamper that Kasey and Kody sent over. It's the first time since I lost Dad that I feel at peace.

The following day is Christmas Eve and just after lunch, I wave off Marlee as she heads to her parents' place for Christmas. She invited me to come with her, but I'm not really in a Christmassy mood, and surprisingly it's not because I'm a Grinch.

Two hours later, I'm sitting on my couch when another crazy idea pops into my head. Grabbing my phone, I make a quick call. Once it's all arranged, I pack a bag, jump in my car, and head off on my adventure.

Three hours later, I pull into the driveway. The house before me reminds me of the McAllister house from *Home Alone*. Outside is decorated with lights and the front lawn looks like a winter wonderland. It's gorgeous.

Climbing out of my car, I walk to the front door and ring the doorbell.

"I'll get it." When I hear her voice, I smile and know I'm where I'm meant to be.

The door swings open and her mouth drops open in shock. "Surprise," I say.

"Gage, what are you doing here?"

"Surprising you."

We stare at one another. She doesn't say anything and I begin to think that maybe I shouldn't have come; then she launches herself at me. Wrapping her legs and arms around me, she kisses me. "I've missed you."

"Babe, it's only been five hours."

"Five hours too long," she mumbles into my neck.

"Marlee, climb off him and come inside. You are letting all the cold air in," her mom says, with a big smile on her face.

Marlee removes herself from me, grabs my hand, and pulls me inside, closing the door behind us. "Mom, this is Gage. Gage, this is my mom, Natalie."

"Pleasure to meet you, Mrs. Adams," I say, outstretching my hand.

"Please call me, Natalie," she says, as she wraps her arms around me for a hug. My eyes bug open in shock. She pulls back and grabs my hands. "I'm sorry about your Dad," she comforts, squeezing me tightly, reminding me of Ma.

"Thank you," I say, not really sure on what the etiquette is when it comes to this.

"Come inside, you must be tired after the long drive." We walk down the hall and into a large open kitchen, which smells amazing. If my nose is right, gingerbread is cooling on the stovetop and there are Christmas cookies baking in the oven.

"I'm not too bad actually. The roads were pretty good, I thought for sure I'd hit some snow but it was clear skies." I take a seat at the breakfast bar and Marlee hands me a glass of wine. "Vermelho?" I whisper.

She grins at me and giggles, just as the sliding door in the dining room opens. An older gentleman walks in. "Wow, the snow is really coming down now." He looks at me and smiles when he sees me sitting at the counter. He walks toward me. "You must be, Gage."

"Yes, I'm Gage. It's a pleasure to finally meet you, sir."

"Please, call me, Roger. You made good time, I wasn't expecting you for a few more hours yet, and with the weather out there, even later."

"Huh?" Marlee asks.

"I kinda gave your dad a heads-up that I was coming."

"Really?" she asks, looking between the two of us.

We both nod our heads. "Dad, you are the worst secret keeper ever."

"Why do you think I've been hiding in the shed all afternoon? I couldn't stand the cold anymore, so I came back inside and was going to take my chances, but what do you know, your surprise was already here." He walks over to Marlee and kisses her head, "Merry Christmas, Pumpkin."

"Merry Christmas, Daddy."

He steps to the window and looks outside. "It's really coming down out there now, how did you get here so quickly?"

"It's was fine. Not one flake fell while I was driving."

"Well, that's great. Can I get you a drink?"

Raising my glass, I say, "I'm all good. Can I help with anything, Mrs. Adams?"

"Natalie, please. And no, you are a guest."

Marlee takes my hand and walks us into the living room. We sit by the fire, drinking our wine and laughing. It's relaxing and I'm glad I made the decision to come; it's just what I needed. Natalie and Rodger come and join us, and the conversation and laughs continue into the wee hours of the morning.

By the time, Marlee and I stumble to bed; we are pretty drunk. We collapse onto the mattress and fall into a drunken slumber.

I'm blissfully woken the next morning with Marlee's lips wrapped around my cock. She stares at me as she sucks me deep into her mouth. When she begins to squeeze my balls and massage that spot at the base of my dick, I come in her mouth. She sucks me dry, and with a pop she removes her mouth and climbs up my body.

"Merry Christmas," she whispers before kissing me.

"Merry Christmas," I whisper back, wrapping my arms around her, holding her close to me.

When her body relaxes, I flip her onto her back and she lets out a yelp. "Shhhh," I whisper, as I drag my nose down her chest. Pushing up her shirt, I kiss her mound through her panties. Breathing in her scent, I rip her panties off her and discard the torn material onto the bed next to us. Running my tongue down her slit, she moans and wriggles beneath me. "You're soaked," I growl as I thrust my tongue into her channel. Licking up and down, I nibble and suck her clit and thrust two fingers into her.

"Gage," she moans, running her fingers through my hair before shoving my face farther into her. Her body tenses, she pulls on my hair and whisper moans, "I'm coming." Her body shudders under me and I continue to thrust my finger in and out until she stills.

Removing my fingers, I bring them to my lips and lick them clean. "MMMM," I moan.

Lying on my back next to her, I stare at the ceiling, happy and content for the first time since I lost Dad. Looking over to her, I smile and cannot wait to give her my real gift later.

We shower separately and make our way downstairs and head to the kitchen. The smell yesterday was amazing, but the scent wafting through the house right now is mouthwatering.

"Merry Christmas, Mom and Dad," Marlee greets as we enter the kitchen.

"Merry Christmas, baby," Natalie says, as she places a tray on top of the stove. She removes the pot holder and throws it on the counter. Walking over to us, she wraps Marlee in a hug and then does the same to me.

"Where's Dad?" Marlee asks, as she pours us each a coffee.

"Stoking the fire." And on cue, he steps into the kitchen.

"Morning," he says, stepping over to Marlee and hugging her.

"Morning, Daddy. Merry Christmas."

"Merry Christmas, Pumpkin." He places a kiss on her forehead and looks to me. "Merry Christmas, Gage," he says, stretching out his hand to me. Placing my hand in his, we shake and stare at one another, he winks at me, knowing what I'm about to give to Marlee.

He slips the box into my hand, and I walk over to

Marlee. "Merry Christmas, babe," I say, placing the box on the counter in front of her. She looks down and her mouth drops open in shock. With shaking hands, she removes the lid on the box, and looks inside. Her mouth pops open again. "Marlee, will you move in with me? I know it's crazy and too soon, but life's too short to not jump in and take risks."

"Yes!" she shouts, wrapping her arms around. Slamming her lips to mine, she kisses me deeply. "I can't wait to get home."

"Home, I like the sounds of that."

I may have been a Christmas Grinch in the past, but Marlee changed all of that. She was a gift sent from Ma, and I don't intend on sharing her anytime soon. She gave me a newfound appreciation for Christmas and a new lease on life…December is now my favorite time of year!

EPILOGUE

The last twelve months have been amazing. So much has happened since last Christmas. Some good. Some bad, and some downright devastating, but I have the most amazing woman by my side, and I know I can survive anything that is thrown at me.

The toy drive is a success and once again, I dress up as Santa. And again, I have a blast, not that I'll tell Kasey and Chelle that. This year though, rather than me dressing sexily as Santa when we arrive home, it's Marlee. Walking into our bedroom, I pause midstep. "Fuck me," I whisper and my cock springs to life.

Standing before me in nothing but a Santa hat, two strategically placed bows, and the sexiest pair of fuck-me heels I have ever seen, is Marlee. "You like?" she huskily whispers.

Nodding my head, I step toward her. Undoing the buttons on my shirt as I go. Sliding the material down my arms, I let it flutter to the carpet. Flipping open the button on my jeans, I push them and my briefs down my legs. I'm now stark naked, standing in front of her. "Can I open my present now?" I asks, my voice deep and full of lust.

With her eyes locked on mine, she shakes her head. But as she does so, she raises her hand and undoes the bow covering her breasts. The red ribbon falls to the floor, lowering my head; I suck a nipple into my mouth and squeeze the other between my thumb and forefinger.

Dropping to my knees, I nuzzle her mound behind the bow. Darting my tongue out, I can't reach where I want, lifting my hand, I undo the bow and smile. "Best. Present. Ever," I say, before I bury my face between her legs. Licking and sucking, I bring her to the brink while I fumble in my pants, when I have what I want in my hand, I stop what I'm doing and raise myself onto one knee.

"Gage!" Marlee protests and when she lowers her gaze to me, her mouth drops open in shock.

"You are the best thing to ever crash into me. You make me a better person each and every day. Without you, I'd still be the cranky Grinch that I once was. Marlee Adams, will you marry me?"

She drops to her knees nodding her head. "Yes. Gage, yes, I will marry you."

Slipping the solitaire diamond onto her ring finger, I grip her cheeks and kiss her deeply. She breaks our kiss and says, "We will need to come up with a PG version of our proposal. We can't tell our kids and everyone that

Mommy and Daddy were naked and Daddy was eating Mommy out when he proposed."

"Mommy and Daddy?" He questions.

"Surprise," she announces. "Merry early Christmas, Gage."

"Best. Christmas. Ever." I say, slamming my lips against my fiancée and the mother of my child's sexy sassy lips. December really is a great month.

EXTENDED EPILOGUE
MARLEE

…February 6th, 2025

Tonight Gage and I are celebrating our fourth wedding anniversary; I can't believe it's been that long already. Some days it feels like we've been married forever, others it's like we only met yesterday. But one thing is still the same; I'm still head over heels in love with Gage Grainger.

He's changed so much since we first met. He was bitter and a total Grinch. He was basically an asshole, but over time, I've chipped away at his black heart—and in return —a man with a heart of gold has emerged. He loves

Amelia and me with everything he has, we are two very lucky gals.

When I crashed—literally—into him, it was unexpected, but to this day, it feels like he was a gift sent to me. My mind drifts to the day we crashed into each other back in 2018...

...Today I'm meeting with Chelle and Kasey at WFOX-FM to work on the annual Christmas drive, we are a last-minute new organization assisting this year, hence the late arrival of me. As the elevator takes me up, my heart rate accelerates with nerves. This is my chance to show my bosses at Chicago Hope that I am the person for this job. It's been my dream to work there for as long as I can remember. The day they offered me the position, I thought all my Christmases had come at once... until I stepped into the foyer of WFOX-FM and crashed into Gage.

Due to my nerves, I wasn't watching where I was going, and I crashed into something hard, something that is now cupping my ass. Lifting my gaze, my hearts stops, it literally stops beating. Holding me in his arms is the sexiest man I have ever seen and he currently has his hand firmly on my ass. When he asked if I was okay, the deep timbre of his voice soaked my panties immediately.

My brain finally kicked into gear and I asked him to remove his hand from my ass. He removed his hand and I took the opportunity to really check him out, unfortunately for me, he caught me and I began to blush profusely.

Somehow I managed to introduce myself, without making a fool of myself, and then I made a hasty exit and headed to my meeting. However, throughout that meeting, my mind kept drifting to the sexy man who groped my ass and set my insides ablaze...

"What are you smiling about, wife?" Gage says, as he walks into our walk-in closet, in nothing but his dress pants.

"Just remembering the day I crashed into you and how you 'accidentally' copped a feel of my ass."

"I swear, it was an accident." He walks over to me and squeezes my ass, "Just like that was an accident." He places a kiss on my shoulder. Just the feel of his lips on my skin sets my body on fire...and I cannot wait for tonight.

"Accident my ass," I tease with a grin as spin to face him. Draping my arms over his shoulders, I gaze into this eyes and see love in his reflecting back to me. He kisses the tip of my nose and winks; I love his playfulness and him, unconditionally. "Are you nearly ready to go?" I ask, as I slip on my emerald green halter dress.

"Nearly," he replies, as he pulls on a charcoal button-down and begins to do up the buttons.

"Well, hurry up," I say as I slip on my heels, "we still need to drop off Amelia."

Kasey and Branson are taking Amelia for the night, and with our alone time, I have some wicked plans in store for my sexy as sin husband...if only he'd hurry up. I swear he takes longer to get ready than I do.

"Thank you so much for this, Kasey, we really appreciate it. It feels like it's been forever since Gage and I have had a night for just us," I tell her as Amelia runs past us, excitedly shouting to KJ and the girls, Gracie and Ginny, that she has arrived. Gage steps past us and places a kiss on her cheek before taking Amelia's things inside.

"It's no problem at all. The girls love playing with Amelia, and they've been so excited for her to come over. What's one extra when I already have three terrors? Four, if I include Branson." We both laugh at her dig at Branson.

Amelia walks back to me and she tugs on my dress. Dropping down to her height, I take her tiny hands in mine. "What's up, baby girl?"

"Juice pwease, Mommy." Her little lisp shining through.

"You have to ask Aunty Kasey, she's the boss tonight."

Amelia looks up at Kasey and smiles. "Juice pwease, Aunty Kwasey."

"How can I can I say no to that? Say bye to Mommy and Daddy, and then we can get you all a juice and maybe even some chippies before dinner."

Her eyes widen in delight. She quickly turns to face Gage and me. "Bye, Mommy and Daddy." She waves, grabs Kasey's hand, and begins to pull her inside, trying to close the door in our face.

"Chips trump us it seems," I joke to Gage.

"I love you more than chips," Gage replies with a wink.

"Get a room, you two," Branson says, as he comes to the door. He kisses my cheek and fists bumps with Gage. I've never understood why men do that, then again, I don't understand a lot of things men do.

"Have a good night, baby girl," I say, blowing her a kiss.

She looks to me and smiles. "Bye, Mommy," she

singsongs, as she continues to pull on Kasey's hand. "Bye, Daddy."

"Have a great night, guys. We will drop her home midmorning," Branson confirms, since Kasey has been accosted by our little monkey.

"Sounds great, and thank you again, we appreciate it."

"Anytime." Branson closes the door and Gage laces his fingers with mine as we walk to the car.

We climb in and it's silent. I look to him. "I miss her already," I quietly admit.

"Me too, but I promise to take your mind off her." He winks at me and then starts the car and we pull out of the driveway.

"So, dear husband of mine, where are you taking me for our anniversary dinner tonight? You and I need to fuel up before I have my wicked way with you all night long."

"If I tell you, then I'd have to kill you, and I'd rather have, how did you just put it? Ohh, yes, I'd rather have my wicked sexy way with you all night long, and for that I need you alive."

"Smart-ass."

"You love my ass."

"No, as I remember it, you love *my* ass."

"Hell yes, I do."

He pulls into the parking lot of Lucio's and my face breaks out into a grin. "Ohh, Gage Grainger, you are so getting lucky tonight."

"If all I have to do is bring you here, I'll bring you here every night of the week."

"Do that, and I'll end up the size of a house."

"But you'd be a sexy as sin house."

"You need your eyes tested, but first I am going to eat my weight in pasta."

We exit the car and walk toward Lucio's. We discovered this place when Stacey was raving about it one day a few years back. I'm so glad she found it because I am now addicted to the gnocchi here. I don't know what Lucio does, but it's velvety smooth and ohh so delicious.

Stepping inside, my senses are assaulted with the yummy Italian goodness, and then I hear in his thick Italian accent, "Signora Grainger." Turning to the voice, I see a beaming Lucio walking over to us. He gently grips my upper arms and air kisses me.

"Lucio, it's so good to see you."

"And you too." He turns to Gage. "You need to bring Signora Grainger here more often." Gage nods. "And where is your lil' bambino this evening?"

"She's at a family friend's place," Gage says, "I wanted to spoil my wife for the evening."

"You have a good man here."

"I sure do," I say, as I look over at my husband and wink. As I gaze at him, I realize I love him just as much today as I did the day I literally fell into him, if not more.

Lucio ushers us to our table and leaves. He quickly returns with wine, Vermelho, and what I like to call the 'Ultimate Italian Antipasto Platter.' The platter has assorted imported Italian meats and cheeses and it's paired with sweet fresh fruit, nuts, bread, marmalade, and a crushed red pepper spread. I could easily eat just this, but I know for the next course, Lucio will bring me his latest gnocchi creation and Gage will have his usual, lasagne.

Wiping my mouth after licking the plate clean—hey, it

was tiramisu—I look to my husband and find him watching me intently. "What?"

"You are just as exquisite today, as you were seven years ago when I first laid eyes on you."

"And you are just as spunky, Mr. Grainger. How about you take me home and I can show you just how much I appreciate you?"

"Check please," he hollers with a laugh, as he leans across the table and places his lips against mine. He holds the back of my head and assaults my mouth with his tongue. "Let's go, Mrs. Grainger, so I can have my wicked way with you."

"Check please," I mimic and stand up, offering my hand to Gage. He places his palm in mine and heat instantly travels through my body. We walk hand in hand to the cashier. We settle the bill, say our goodbyes to Lucio, and head home for what I know will be a sexy good night.

♡

EXTENDED EPILOGUE
GAGE

As I sit next to my wife in the car on the way home, I glance over at her and to this day, I still cannot believe that she's in my life. She is a gift I will cherish forever. She and Amelia mean everything to me. Sure, I'd love to have a son, but Marlee had a really rough delivery with Amelia, and I would not wish that upon her, or me, again. And that's fine by me, I have two beautiful angels to spoil each and every day, and I could not be happier.

Parking in the garage, we head inside, and as soon the door is closed behind me, my wife pushes me against the wood and covers my mouth with hers. She slides her tongue along my lips, slipping it inside my mouth. I moan into her mouth, as I grip her ass—her sexy as sin ass—and knead her ass cheeks in my palms. Tapping her ass, she instinctively jumps up and wraps her legs around my waist, grinding herself on my hardening cock.

Racing into our bedroom, I lower her to the floor at the end of the bed. She stares at me as she reaches to her neck and unties the bow of her halter dress. The material slides down her body, and flutters to the floor. Leaving her in her heels and a lingerie set that is sexy as hell; thank you *Agent Provocateur*.

"Marlee," I whisper, as I trace my finger across the top of her strapless bra, "What am I going to do with you?"

"I have a few ideas," she huskily replies, as she begins to pop open the buttons on my shirt. She becomes restless and tears at it, buttons flying about the room. I look at her questioningly.

"What?" she innocently replies with a shrug of her shoulders. With a smirk, she slides the material down my arms before dropping it to the floor next to her discarded dress. She makes quick work of my pants and as she slides them and my briefs down my legs, she drops to her knees and takes my cock in her mouth. With her eyes fused to mine, she slides my shaft in and out of her mouth. Lifting her hand, she cups my balls and gently massages them. Out of nowhere, I explode in her mouth. My hot salty seed slides down her throat and she drinks every milky drop. Pulling my cock out of her mouth, she wipes at her lips, sliding her finger into her mouth and sucking.

Reaching down, I lift her up and slam my lips against hers. Threading my fingers into her hair, I fuck her mouth with my tongue. Sitting on the edge of the bed, she straddles me. Reaching behind her, she unclasps her bra, dropping it on top of our clothes. Gripping the sides of her panties, I tear them from her body, her eyes pop open at this. "Hey," she scolds, "I like that set."

"I'll buy you another," I affirm before I press my lips to her. She lifts her hips and hovers above my cock. Even though I just came, it's rock-hard once again. Marlee has that effect on me, never have I felt like this with anyone before, and all these years later, she still owns my heart.

Ever so slowly, she slides down my cock. Impaling herself. When she's fully seated on me, she grips my shoulders and begins to ride me. Grasping her hips tightly in my hands, she continues to thrust up and down. My fingers digging deeper with each gyration. She grips her tits and massages them, pinching her nipples between her thumb and forefinger. Leaning forward, I take one into my mouth and suck, garnering a guttural moan from her. Biting the tip, she screams and topples over the edge. Panting and moaning through her climax, she opens her eyes and winks at me, this causes me to explode and I come, spilling my seed inside her.

Flopping back to the mattress, she lies beside me. Her head resting on my chest. Her breathing eventually evens out and I know she's sounds asleep, snuggled into me. It just so happens to be my favorite position to fall asleep in.

Absentmindedly, I run my fingers through her silky locks and stare down at my gorgeous sleeping wife. My last thought, before I drift off to sleep, is how she was an unexpected gift I never knew I wanted or needed. I will treasure the gift of her, and Amelia, for the rest of my days.

THE END!!!!!

Read on for a sneak peek at The Unexpected Letter.

CHAPTER 1

… May 5th, 2019

MY GIRLFRIENDS HAVE SURPRISED ME WITH A BACHELORETTE weekend away…to Kansas, of all places, but Stacey assures me that it's 'totally worth the trip.' I'm yet to see that, or anything, because I'm currently blindfolded, sitting in the back of a stretch Hummer.

The bubbly is flowing. The laughs are a plenty and the atmosphere is electric, and everyone is having fun; blindfolded me included.

The car stops and a few moments later the driver opens the door. "Ladies, you have arrived," he says, as he takes my hand and helps me out. It's really disorientating being blindfolded but at the same time it's exhilarating and exciting. It reminds me of my birthday last year...

...February 27th, 2018

"Branson, where are you taking me and WHY the friggin' hell am I blindfolded?"

"Because!" he playfully replies.

"Because? Really? That's all I get?"

"Yep. Now get in, and watch your head. If you turn up injured, Kody will kick my ass."

"I'll kick your ass for not telling me where we are going."

"I'd like to see you try." He pauses and I can tell he's grinning right now. "Now get in."

"You're a bossy boots," I huff.

"Says the queen of bossy."

"I'm not bossy," I scoff, whacking the air—hoping to get Branson—but instead my knuckles hit the car door. "Shit!" I shout, shaking my hand to ease the pain.

Suddenly, my hand is enveloped in warmth and I feel soft lips pressed against my knuckles. "There all better," Branson huskily whispers.

"My hero," I singsong.

"If it wasn't your birthday, I'd totally smack your ass for being cheeky."

"Maybe I want to be smacked," I mischievously reply.

It's suddenly silent, the only sound to be heard is each of us breathing. It's awkward but not, the moment is broken when Branson taps my side. "Come on, we better get going, otherwise you'll be late."

"Late for what?" I question.

"Wouldn't you like to know?"

"Umm, yes, that's why I asked."

"Shut up and get in, birthday brat."

Just like that, Branson and I are back to our usual playful selves. With a smile, I carefully climb in and await my surprise. We don't drive for long and when we arrive, Branson tells me to wait there—like I'm going to go anywhere on my own blindfolded. The car door opens and Branson carefully escorts me out of the vehicle, down a walkway, through several doors, and then we stop. Branson lifts my blindfold off and I'm met with a chorus of "Surprise" and "Happy Birthday," deafening cheers and claps.

My eyes lock on Kody's and I smile. He saunters over to me, wrapping his arms around my waist. "Happy birthday, *gorgeous!" he says, before he plants a searing hot kiss on my lips.*

Pulling back, I grip both his hands and squeeze. "Thanks for this, babe, it was totally unexpected."

"Don't thank me, thank him." He points to Branson, who is smiling sheepishly from behind us.

Stepping over to Branson, I kiss him on the cheek and hug him, "Thank you Branson."

He hugs me back and quietly murmurs, "Your welcome, Kase. I'd do anything to see you happy. Happy birthday."

He steps back and walks over to his parents, just as Kody wraps his arms around me from behind. He nuzzles my neck and whispers, "Make sure you keep that blindfold, I'm getting all sorts of kinky sexy ideas for later."

Spinning around, I give him a wink. "You had me a kinky." I kiss his jaw, blissfully happy at my surprise party and totally in love with Kody Holmes…

Remembering that night, I squeeze my thighs together and decide I'm TOTALLY keeping this blindfold for when I get home, Kody and I are going to have some blindfolded fun…again.

"What are you grinning about?" Stacey asks me.

"Nothing, I'm just really excited for the night ahead."

"Mmmhmpf." I know that tone from her, she doesn't believe me at all, but thankfully she doesn't push me. With a sigh, I stand on the pavement, blindfolded, and wait while the girls all climb out. Suddenly, there are hands on my shoulders, and Stacey says from behind me, "Let's go." She pushes me forward. "Okay, babe, there are," she pauses for a bit, "seven steps and then the fun is going to begin."

Somehow, I make it up the stairs without tripping, or breaking anything. I'm grinning when a deep husky voice says, "Welcome, ladies. My name is Marcus, let me know if I can be of any assistance this evening."

"You can tell me where I am?" I ask.

He takes my hand and kisses the back of it. "Nice try, Kasey. Just go with the flow and enjoy yourself." With my sight gone, his voice is prominent and ohh so fine…*I bet he's butt-ugly,* I think to myself and giggle as I'm pushed farther into the establishment.

"You know my name?" I ask, but I'm met with silence.

We stop walking again and Stacey says, "Well, der, of course, you are the main star tonight," I swear she silently adds, "except for those up on stage." This piques my curiosity.

"Oooookay," I offer in reply.

Stacey is now quietly talking to someone and I'm left alone, blindfolded in the middle of, I don't know where in Kanas. I shake my head and again giggle to myself.

"Let's go," Stacey suddenly says, a door opens, and we walk inside. There's music thumping. Women are chattering and giggling. Glasses are clinking and I'm now guessing we are in a bar. We stop suddenly and Stace lifts off my blindfold. Blinking a few times, my vision comes back, and I look to Stacey, she's grinning from ear to ear and raises her eyebrows seductively at me before she excitedly screams, "Welcome to Bare Chested!"

"Huh?" I ask confused.

"We will be seeing our very own sexy schmexy strip show…right after Marcus here," she flicks her eyes to the left where I see a sexy as sin guy hungrily staring and walking toward me, "gives you an up close and personal lap dance."

My mouth drops open in shock. I remember mentioning to Stace that I have always wanted to go to a strip club, but I never expected this. "Stacey," I say, my eyes well with tears.

"Nope, no crying." She shakes her head. "Now, sit back and enjoy." She pushes my shoulders and I drop down on to the seat. My phone rings and it's Branson's tone. "Nope, he can wait," Stacey says, as she hands me another shot, I throw it back and shrug, after all, who am I to argue when a sexy guy is prowling toward me.

"WooooHooooo," I shout, as he saunters over to me.

A glass of bubbly is thrust into my hand; I drink the entire thing and slam the empty glass onto the table next to me. Marcus is now in front of me, grinding his hips in circles. "This is so hot," I giggle as he rests his hands on the couch arms, cocooning me.

"Hey."

"Hey," I giggle in reply, yes, I giggle like a schoolgirl. Suddenly the bubbly from the limo and the shot I just skulled hit me with force. My phone rings again, but before I can say anything, Stacey digs it out and silences it.

Marcus grabs my chin and turns my attention back to him. He sexily spins about and now has his back to me, shaking his tight sexy ass in my face. Leaning forward, I mimic licking when he reaches behind him, grabs my hands and pulls me forward. My face is pressed against his back and he runs my hands up and down his abs. Holy muscles, Batman, I throw my head back and laugh. The girls all laugh and smile. This is so fun and so sexy at the same time, *I wonder if I can persuade Kody to do something like this for me when I get home?*

All too soon, my dance is over. Marcus lifts my hand and places a kiss on the back, just like when we arrived. "You will make a beautiful bride," he says, before turning and sauntering away.

Another glass of bubbly appears, and I drink it slowly. I look around; everyone is smiling, laughing, and having the best time. "Stacey, this is awesome and the best night ever." I pause and swallow the lump in my throat. "Thanks so much."

The lights on the stage dim and she leans into me and whispers, "The fun is just starting, babe."

A song I don't recognize begins to play and the sexiest guy ever struts his stuff on stage in nothing but black pants and a tie…and he wears the hell out of that tie. I scream and holler like the others in the club. He introduces himself as Jake and then he's asking about a bachelorette party and starts walking down the stage stairs. He comes over to us, his eyes are locked on Karen, her face turns beet red. "Are you the lucky lady whose getting married?" His voice is deep and ohh so sexy.

Karen turns to me, grabs my wrist, and shouts, "No, but she is," as she shoves me toward him.

"Well, aren't you a beautiful woman?" he croons. "Your soon-to-be husband is a lucky man." He takes my hand, pulls out a chair, and gently pushes me down to take a seat. He spins around and shakes his ass in my face, once again I giggle and laugh. Someone yells for me to squeeze his butt, I'd really like to, but I'm not sure of the protocol in a club like this, so I keep my hands in my lap. But my eyes travel all over this body. There isn't an ounce of fat on him, and he has muscles that I have never seen up close before.

He spins back to face me and grabs my hands, running them up and down his abs…his rock-hard abs. My eyes land on his and he winks at me, just as I hear Stacey yelling my name. Turing to face her, I see tears welling in her eyes. She holds the phone to my ear. "Hello," I breathlessly say into the phone.

"Kace, it's Branson." Instantly, my body freezes, his tone is off.

"What's wrong?" I ask, I hold my breath and wait for his reply. Without him saying anything, I know it's bad news.

"Kody…"

"No, no, no." I say into the phone, shoving Jake away with all my might, he stumbles backward as I stand up. "…he didn't make it." I'm frozen on the spot, I shake my head from side to side as tears cascade down my cheeks; everything around me fades out. Branson is talking but I don't hear anything. In my head, over and over I just keep repeating the last thing I clearly heard Branson say to me 'he didn't make it.'

A guttural scream passes my lips. Falling to my knees, I drop the phone and collapse into a heap. Everything around me goes silent; Stacey squats down and rubs my back. I can feel everyone's gaze on me but I feel so alone right in this moment. My heart is shattering into a million fragments. My life will be altered from this moment forward. From next to me I hear Stacey say over and over, "Shit, shit, shit."

She wraps her arms around me and pulls me into her

chest as the world around me crumbles. "Kasey, babe. I'm so sorry."

"What's going on?" Karen asks.

Looking up at her, I don't know what to say. My heads starts shaking from side to side again and I cover my mouth, as a fresh batch of tears fall.

Stacey looks over at her and sadly says, "It's Kody. He's dead."

The Unexpected Letter is out 10th November.

ACKNOWLEDGMENTS

My betas babe, **Halle, Amanda, Beth** and **Crissy**. Sorry for making you cry (#SorryNotSorry) but I do appreciate your feedback, support and everything that you do for me.

Dana Leah from **Designs by Dana**, you took my idea and picture and turned it into something amazing. Thank you so much, I love the cover. It was awesome to work with you.

Karen Hrdlicka from **Barren Acres Editing**, once again thank you for combing through my MS and helping me make it the best that it can be. I love working with you.

And, finally, **you, my reader**. Thanks for coming along for the ride, and if you are new to me, welcome aboard. I hope you enjoyed my naughty Grinch, here's to many more stories together.

Wine Not (Book 3)

The Final Shot (Book 4)

The Liquor Cabinet: Series boxset

STAND ALONES

Out of Nowhere

Antecedent

Seven Nights

Falling for Dr. Kelly, a Falling novel

Falling for Dr. Knight, a Falling novel - coming May 2020

Doc Steel - coming June 2020

The Dirty Dozen: Alpha edition

The Rule Breaker Anthology - coming soon

In the Dark of Night anthology (only available in paperback directly from me)

Titanic Tales, a charity anthology (no longer available)

Gone Coastal, a sizzling summer beach anthology (no longer available)

Leave Me Breathless: The Lilac Collection (no longer available)

ABOUT THE AUTHOR

DL Gallie is from Queensland, Australia, but she's lived in many different places all over the world, including the UK and Canada. She currently resides in Central Queensland with her husband and two munchkins. She and her husband have been together since she was sixteen, and although they drive each other crazy at times, she couldn't imagine her life without him.

Shortly after her son was born, DL began reading again. With encouragement from her husband, she picked up the pen and started writing, and now the voices in her head won't shut up.

DL enjoys listening to music, drinking white wine in the summer, red wine in the winter, and beer all year round. She's also never been known to turn down a cocktail, especially a margarita.